Mills & Boon
Best Seller Romance

A chance to read and collect some of the best-loved novels
from Mills & Boon—the world's largest publisher of
romantic fiction.

Every month, four titles by favourite Mills & Boon authors
will be re-published in the *Best Seller Romance* series.

A list of other titles in the *Best Seller Romance* series
can be found at the end of this book.

Charlotte Lamb

THE LONG SURRENDER

MILLS & BOON LIMITED
LONDON · TORONTO

First published 1978
Australian copyright 1978
Philippine copyright 1978
This edition 1984

© Charlotte Lamb 1978

ISBN 0 263 74587 2

Set in Linotype Baskerville 10 on 11½ pt.
02-0284

*Made and printed in Great Britain by
Richard Clay (The Chaucer Press) Ltd,
Bungay, Suffolk*

CHAPTER ONE

SELINA was in the bathroom when she heard the letter-box rattle, followed by the thud of the newspaper hitting the hall floor. She went on cleaning her teeth vigorously, her slanting green eyes fixed on her reflection. It was time to make an appointment with the hairdresser, she decided. Her hair was growing out of the style she preferred. Although she usually had it professionally styled once every couple of months, she washed and set it herself on heated rollers to get the casual, loose fashion she liked, the red-gold curls sweeping down around her high-cheekboned face to soften a faint angularity of profile.

When she had rinsed her mouth she stepped on to the bathroom scales, surveyed the swinging needle with satisfaction, then moved towards the bathroom door, tying the belt of her loose silk wrapper more tightly.

She paused in the hall to pick up the newspaper from the mat, put it under her arm and went through into the tiny kitchen, yawning. She was up earlier than usual because she had been able to get an early night for once, but she still felt slightly sleepy. Opening the refrigerator, she took out a jug of chilled orange juice, poured some into a glass, switched off the percolator which was hitting its glass dome excitedly, slid a slice of bread into the toaster and sat down. Her movements all had a ritual deliberation. She did this every morning

5

and had cut every unnecessary action until the whole process only took a few moments.

Taking a sip of her orange juice, she casually flipped open the front page of the newspaper and glanced at it. As she took in the main headline her hand began to shake. The glass fell to the floor, shattering, sending a stream of orange juice seeping over her fluffy white slippers.

'No!' she whispered huskily, shaking her head in an automatic, unconscious gesture of rejection. 'No, it isn't true . . .'

Feverishly she skimmed the story, her lips trembling as she read. An aeroplane had crashed in the mountains of Peru, killing everyone on board, including three people whose names were world-famous. There were small photographs of the three, but it was on the second picture that her eyes were riveted. The colour had slowly drained from her face until she was as white as the wrapper she wore. Her toast popped up unheeded. Orange juice soaked the white fur slippers, ruining them for ever. Her lips were parted, murmuring a name.

When the telephone in the hall rang she jumped violently, brushing a hand across her eyes. Her fingers came away wet. For a moment she sat quite still, taking a deep breath, then very slowly she walked out into the hall and picked up the shrilling receiver.

'Yes?' Her voice sounded rusty, as thought she had forgotten how to speak.

'Selina, it's Roger. Have you seen today's newspaper yet?' The voice was hurried and anxious.

'Yes,' she said dully.

There was a pause. 'Are you all right?' The question

came sharply. 'It's quite a shock, isn't it? I couldn't believe it until I'd read it a couple of times. Would you like me to come over? I can get the morning off.'

'No,' she said flatly. 'There's no need to do that.'

'Are you sure? Look, they won't mind when I tell them that my sister's husband has been killed in an accident ...'

'Ex-husband,' she said. 'We were divorced, Roger. Ex-husband.'

'Well, yes,' he said uncomfortably. 'But it must still be a shock to you.'

'Yes.' The admission was made huskily. She wished he would get off the line. The tears just would not stop and she was afraid she would break down unmistakably any moment. She did not want even Roger to know how badly this had hit her.

'If you hadn't divorced him you'd be a very wealthy widow,' Roger said wistfully.

'For God's sake!' Her voice broke and she flushed with sudden shocked anger. 'How can you think about money at such a time?'

'It's only human to realise that Ashley must have left someone a great deal of money,' he said, half in deprecation, half in defiance. 'I see Clare Leslie died in the crash, too. So she won't be getting his money. What was she like?'

'Beautiful,' Selina said on a harsh note she couldn't control. It was absurd that she should still feel that deep, bitter pang of jealousy. It was three years ago and now he was dead, and the fact of a world in which Ashley no longer existed was intolerable.

'If Ashley fell for her she would obviously be something special,' Roger said casually.

Roger had always been totally without sensitivity, Selina thought angrily; apparently it never occurred to him that every word he said might be pressing on an unhealed scar.

'I must go,' she said calmly. 'I've got a lot to do to-day.'

'Oh,' he said, surprised. 'I just wanted to check you were okay.'

'I am, thank you,' she said carefully.

'After all, you're my kid sister,' he said brightly.

She laughed slightly at that. She had never been able to stay angry with Roger for long, even though she was well aware that he had a selfish streak in his nature which made him occasionally incredibly callous and unaware of the feelings of other people. They had to stick together. They had no one else in the world but each other. They had been through so much together and it had welded them into a strong unit. Roger knew he could always rely on her.

'You've got that the wrong way round,' she pointed out. 'You are my kid brother. I've got the edge on you, remember. I'm the eldest.'

'Same thing,' he said lightly. 'Pity about the money, though. I could have done with a miracle.'

She picked up the hint at once, as no doubt he had expected her to. 'Roger, you haven't been gambling?' Her voice held panic and alarm.

He ignored the question. 'I suppose Ashley won't have left you anything in his will? For old times' sake? I mean, he was pretty crazy about you and you were the one who wanted the divorce. He may not have altered his will.'

Her temper flared. 'You don't think I'd take his

money, even if he had left me any? I wouldn't touch it with a bargepole!'

'Sis, you've got to be kidding,' he gasped. 'Don't talk like that!'

The vehemence in his voice made her alarm grow stronger. 'Roger, how much do you owe this time?'

'We'll talk later,' he said. 'I must fly. See you, Sis,' and the telephone went dead.

Selina replaced the receiver slowly and stood staring down into the black pit of time, remembering things she had thought buried for ever.

Ashley ...

Her mouth shaped the name silently, a moan wrenching her as she tried to accept his death.

She walked back into the kitchen, struggling with tears, and stood at the sink, breathing with the controlled rhythm of the singer. It always helped to force down emotions. After a while the ragged agony eased and she turned away to pour herself a cup of coffee.

He had never married Clare, apparently, although they must have been travelling together. It could not be a coincidence that they were both on that plane. Presumably one marriage had been enough for Ashley. He had been a wary, sophisticated bachelor when they met, his every instinct suspicious of matrimonial entanglement. No doubt their brief and hellish experience had confirmed his low opinion of that state, as it had her own. She knew she would never marry again; her months with Ashley had made that certain.

Two cups of coffee later she felt able to get dressed. She dropped the uneaten slice of toast into the bin, washed up and dried up, put the breakfast things away. Despite her misery it helped to stick to her usual morning routine. She liked to keep the flat tidy and being busy would stop her thinking.

She unconsciously chose a quiet grey dress to wear, a muted colour which reflected her mood, and made up carefully. She had just finished when the telephone rang again. She hesitated before answering it. It had just occurred to her that some journalist with a long memory might have dug her name and address out of his files.

But it was Freddie, his voice filled with warm concern. 'Angel, if you don't want to go on tonight, that's fine by me. I'll find a replacement.'

'No, thanks, Freddie,' she said. 'I'll be fine.'

'Sure, baby?' Freddie knew her too well not to guess how this would hit her. She had begun to sing at Freddie's Place as a schoolgirl of sixteen, a scared, ambitious, shivering teenager in a borrowed dress which didn't quite fit her properly. In the last three years her career had really taken off. Her agent had got her some exciting bookings, including a long run last winter in a Christmas pantomime in a northern seaside resort. He was not talking of jobs in America, and she felt she was beginning to make a name for herself. But she always did a few nights at Freddie's Place now and then, for old times' sake, and she was glad she was singing there at the moment. Freddie was the one person who really understood how she felt about Ashley.

'I'll go on, Freddie,' she said firmly. 'I would rather be working. It will help.'

'Just like the lady says,' he murmured. A pause. 'Bad way for him to go. I'm very sorry, Selina. I admired the guy.'

'Yes,' she said huskily.

'I would have rung you earlier, but I thought it would be best if I gave you time to get over the shock.'

'It was a shock,' she said, understating the case.

'You can say that again! Seems incredible that he's dead ...'

Her breath caught in a spasm of raw agony, and Freddie clicked his tongue apologetically.

'God, I'm sorry, Selina. I'm an idiot.'

'No,' she said, recovering herself. 'You said what was in your mind. It seems incredible to me, too.' And the finality of it was worse than anything. There would never be another chance to see him, hear his voice. She had thought for years that she could not bear to set eyes on Ashley again, but now she knew that never to be able to do so was far worse. There had always been a wall between them. Now there was an abyss she could never cross.

When Freddie had said goodbye she walked into her sitting-room. The flat had a view of the Thames. She had taken the lease for ten years. At first she had barely been able to afford it, but now she was finding money easier and was glad she had risked taking such an expensive flat just because she fell in love with the view.

Today the river was as grey as the autumn sky. Office blocks, church spires and distant factory chimneys gave an irregular edging to the horizon. A few seagulls skimmed along the choppy water, their yellow beaks a splash of brave colour against the prevailing greyness. Two Thames barges chugged past, tarpaulin-draped. A police motor launch swung round to follow them, a uniformed officer standing in the prow with binoculars levelled along the river.

Another normal day for London, Selina thought bitterly. Nothing much happening. Everything quiet. And Ashley Dent lying somewhere on the snow-covered slopes of a South American mountain, his black hair blowing in an icy wind, among the splintered wreckage of an air crash.

She always did her shopping in a busy supermarket nearby, searching carefully along the shelves for the best buys. She had had the sort of upbringing which encourages thrift, and it was a habit she found it hard to forget now that she was earning quite well.

She stopped for a cup of coffee afterwards in a noisy, brightly lit café, wincing at the gaudy surroundings which seemed more than usually intrusive today.

On her way back to the flat she passed a poster. Air crash! The headline leapt out at her. She averted her head, her red-gold hair swinging smoothly against her pale face. Although she wore a fur-trimmed coat the wind made her shiver, and her hands and feet were ice-cold.

Outside the block of flats she met a neighbour who stopped to have a chat, her curious eyes admiring Selina's coat. 'Where are you working this week?' she asked.

'A nightclub in Mayfair,' Selina replied coolly, aware she was the object of gossip among her neighbours.

'Really?' The other woman's eyes widened. Just as Selina was walking away she was suddenly called back. 'Ooh, I forgot ... a reporter was here looking for you. He's gone now.' The avid eyes assessed her again. 'Didn't say what he wanted.'

Selina went into the building, her heart sinking. A reporter ... no prizes to guess what he wanted. They had dug up the divorce reports, of course. Ghouls!

She ate a light lunch of salad and cottage cheese, then settled down to read a book for an hour. It was difficult to concentrate on the pages. At four her agent rang to have a chat. He had seen the papers, too, but he was only marginally interested. 'Any of the press been around?' he wanted to know. She told him that she had missed one, and he made a noncommittal noise.

'Can't make up my mind whether the publicity would be good or bad,' he said thoughtfully. 'You weren't known when the divorce went through. People probably think you've always been single—nice image. A divorce ... well, we'll play it by ear.'

When he had rung off Selina looked out of the window at the darkening sky. Her slender shoulders shook as the tears came again, but she pulled herself together and switched on the television. Anything was better than thinking.

Mindlessly she watched a very unfunny comedy show, then sat through a long current affairs programme, reluctant to get up and switch off.

At last she sighed, forced to do something. She would get to Freddie's a little early tonight. The flat was becoming claustrophobic and she needed to get out of it.

Two hours later she was in her cubbyhole dressing-room at Freddie's Place, slowly applying her make-up, when Freddie put his head round the door.

'How's my princess?' He was a short, thin man of fifty, with greying hair and a clever, shrewd, lived-in face which could keep a secret better than a safe and had very little to learn about life.

She smiled at him, fluttering her curling black false eyelashes. 'You tell me,' she said, very lightly.

He surveyed her in the mirror, his sad monkey eyes kind. 'You've done a great job with the cover-up, Princess,' he told her. 'Still sure you want to go on?'

'You make me feel haggard,' she said, with a forced smile.

'You look as ravishing as ever,' he shrugged. 'Outside.'

'And inside?'

'I'm sorry, Selina.' He came forward to lay both hands on her slender shoulders, his palms warm against her naked skin. 'Chin up, kid.'

She smiled at him, screwing her head round to look up into his eyes. 'I'll be fine.'

'Sure you will,' he said. 'There's a packed house out there, ravening wolves to the last man. When they see you in that dress I'll have to put up iron railings to keep them off!'

'Good business,' she smiled.

'Good of you to come,' he said. 'I know you get better offers. I wish I could match them, but I don't make that sort of money.'

'I know what you make,' she said gently. 'This is for old times' sake. I owe you more than I can ever repay.'

'You don't owe me nothing.'

'You gave me my start in the business.'

'I should have been shot,' he said. 'Giving a little kid of your age to those wolves of mine.'

'I was grateful—still am. I needed the money.'

His eyes were serious. 'Yeah, I know. And he's still bleeding you white.'

She flushed angrily. 'Freddie! Don't talk about Roger like that. It isn't fair. He means well.'

'Sure he does. When are you going to realise, honey,

that brother of yours is addicted to gambling? He's well and truly hooked. As long as you keep feeding him the bread he'll keep gambling.'

'I know,' she said, sighing, her head sinking on her slim white neck. 'But what can I do? You know what happened when I refused to pay.'

'A few beatings like that and he might lose the habit,' Freddie said without confidence.

'A few beatings like that and he might not live to reproach me,' she said bitterly. 'Roger can't take that sort of treatment. He had too much of it as a little boy.'

Freddie sighed deeply, shaking his head. 'That stepfather of yours was a real bastard, one of the worst. The day he died I declared a public holiday.'

Selina was white with terrible memories, her green eyes fierce and savage against her pure skin. 'Don't remind me!' She stood up with a rippling movement and faced him. 'Time to go on.'

Freddie stared at her in riveted admiration. 'How does that damned thing stay up?'

'Will power,' she grinned. As she moved towards the door her slenderly curved body rippled sinuously under the skin-tight black silk dress. There was no back to the gown, and very little front. The black silk cupped her breasts, half revealing them, then curved in to her waist and down over her hips and thighs.

'You forgot your gloves,' said Freddie, picking them up from the dressing-table and tossing them to her.

Selina made a face. 'I do that every night!'

'Freudian slip,' Freddie teased.

She grinned, sliding her fingers into the gloves. They came halfway up her arm, giving her nakedness a strangely exciting formality.

She walked out on to the small stage in darkness. When she was positioned, leaning against the small white piano, a spotlight picked her out. The audience burst into applause, then quietened. She had her back to them, her golden skin glowing like a peach under the blue light. Slowly she turned to face them, her body swaying sensuously, the long black gloves emphasising her smouldering sexuality. The pianist began to play and she started singing. When she began to strip off her gloves, with leisurely provocation, the audience erupted into wolf whistles, stamping their feet. Selina moved across the stage, twirling a glove, and threw it into the darkness. A hand came up to catch it. The audience laughed and whistled again. 'More,' they shouted. 'More!'

Optimists! she thought, finishing the song. As she took her applause, smiling, her eyes swung round the semi-circle of smiling faces and froze as through the smoky darkness she saw a face ... a grim, unsmiling face, with heavy lids half lowered against cigar smoke, steely grey eyes that stabbed at her across the room, and a hard, controlled but sensual mouth.

Selina slid slowly and silently to the floor.

When she opened her eyes again she was lying on the tiny sofa in her dressing-room. She sighed, frowning. What had happened? Suddenly she remembered and began to struggle up.

A hand pushed her back. She stared upwards, a wave of icy coldness washing over her. No ghost, she realised, staring at the tall, lean figure. The thick black hair was tinged with silver and cut in a leonine fashion down past the ears, brushing the white collar of his shirt. The broad shoulders fitted superbly beneath the well-cut dinner jacket.

'You—you're alive,' she stammered.

He inclined his head.

'But the crash ... no survivors, they said ...'

'I was never on the plane. I had to alter my arrangements at the last moment.'

'Oh ...' She was wordless. There seemed no possible response. The deep, singing relief made her feel sick. She lay back, breathing hard, taking in his presence as if it were a fragrance. Then she thought of something and looked up. 'Clare?'

'She was on it,' he said succinctly.

'Oh ...' she said again, quivering. 'I'm sorry.'

'Are you?' The question was contemptuous.

'Yes!' Her reply was low and angry. She stared at him with bitter dislike. Already the grief of her reaction to news of his death was being converted into the old hostility, as though his physical presence provoked a chemical reaction she was unable to control.

'You loathed her,' he said flatly.

'Not that much,' she said. 'Not enough to be glad she's dead.'

His eyes narrowed. 'As you were at the news of my death, no doubt,' he said unpleasantly.

She made no response to that. Not for worlds would she have him suspect her real reaction. She swung her feet down to the ground to sit up, only to find her head going round.

'Stay where you are,' he said roughly, pushing her back against the cushions.

'Don't touch me!' The words flew out before she could stop them, breathless with panic.

His body tensed. His smile grew savage. 'Sorry, I'd forgotten you were untouchable.' The grey eyes slid down her body, stripping her insolently. 'Out there in the spotlight they see a different girl, don't they? You've changed your act since I last saw it. I couldn't believe it was you at first. Who's been giving you lessons? Every movement shouted sex ... that swaying walk, the black silk dress that reveals a hell of a lot more than it conceals, the way you smiled at them.'

'Shut up!' Selina muttered in a smothered voice, bending her head to hide her expression.

'What's the matter, Selina?' he asked silkily. 'You're not ashamed of the way you sell yourself to the audience, are you? Don't try to kid me it wasn't deliberate. Every movement was carefully thought out and rehearsed. When you started taking off those gloves the temperature shot up in there. They were breathless with excitement. Every damned one of them was imagining the rest of your clothes coming off.'

'Damn you!' she said furiously. 'Stop it!'

'I was as mesmerised as the rest of them,' he drawled, ignoring her protest. 'But I had an advantage over them. I've seen all your clothes come off, remember, and the memory was tantalising.'

She flushed scarlet and leapt to her feet to face him, her eyes hating him. 'You bastard! Have you forgotten Clare was killed only yesterday? What were you doing out front tonight?'

'Clare and I split up over two years ago,' he said levelly, the grey eyes freezing over. 'Not that it's any of your business, but strictly for the record.'

'You don't change, do you?' she whispered, staring at him. 'You always used to say ... another woman, another day ... your favourite motto!'

'We neither of us change,' he said flatly. His eyes watched her closely. 'Do we, Selina?'

'Who's the latest woman in your life, Ashley?' she retorted to avoid the question in his eyes.

He shrugged. 'At present, no one.'

She laughed. 'Do you expect me to believe that?'

'Why should I lie?' His tone was casual. 'You wouldn't give a damn if I had a whole harem, would you?'

'I'd be sorry for them,' she said.

As if her reply stung him, he turned away. 'Get out of that dress,' he said crisply.

For one split second she was in a state of mindless panic, her eyes widening, her body gripped by terror.

Ashley turned back and saw her face, his eyes widening, too, then a grim look came into the powerfully moulded features.

'Get changed,' he said flatly. 'I'll wait outside and run you home.'

'I'd prefer to take a taxi,' she protested.

'Too bad.' His mouth set like a trap. 'I want to talk to you.'

'But I don't want to talk to you,' she said huskily. 'We've got nothing to say to each other.'

'After three years?' he asked harshly.

'After an eternity,' she said, her voice low.

'Surely you can bear to sit in a car with me for ten minutes,' he bit out.

'No,' she said, her tone stark and uncompromising. 'I can't.'

There was a silence. Selina looked up and found Ashley watching her out of narrowed, intent eyes. Something in his look made her flush hotly. She turned her back on him, pretending to rearrange the things on her dressing-table, her red-gold head bent to examine a small doll Freddie had given her years ago, and which she had kept ever since as a mascot.

'Close the door as you go out,' she said drily. 'I don't want any more uninvited visitors.'

He did not answer and he made no move, although she listened intently for a sound. Dry-mouthed and nervous, she smoothed down a fold of the black dress. 'Goodnight,' she said, about to turn and stare him down.

Then she felt him right behind her. A flare of terror lit her mind, like lightning splitting a dark sky. One hand clamped her back against his body while the other moved to her zip.

'Don't ...!' Her smothered cry of protest came involuntarily, but his fingers had already slid the zip down until her dress began to fall away from her.

She grabbed at the material, just as his hands pulled her arms backward to tether her in position. The black silk rustled and fell to her feet.

'Not quite as gracefully as it could be done,' he said sardonically. 'You look better without your clothes on, though.'

In the mirror his grey eyes met her frightened, angry green ones. Deliberately he bent and pressed his mouth against her bare shoulder. She felt it like a searing burn and gasped.

'Don't,' she whispered, shivering uncontrollably.

He released her arms, but only in order to slide his hands round her body, warm against her silky underslip, until they cupped her breasts, his mouth searching along her white throat, his eyes still holding hers in the mirror.

'I hate you to touch me,' she flung at him savagely. 'I hate it!'

'Do you, Selina?' The question was unsteady as his mouth moved along her uplifted neck towards her chin. She was rigid against him, her throat flung tautly back to avoid his kiss, deeply aware that he was moving towards her lips.

'Stop it,' she groaned, shuddering. 'Please, stop it!'

His head came up. The hard, masculine face grew darker as he stared at her in the mirror, taking in her tense position, the distaste in the green eyes.

'You little bitch,' he bit out between teeth which snapped together like a steel trap. 'Some day I'll throttle you!' The strong brown hands encircled her throat as if he meant to fulfil the threat there and then. Selina began to shake so violently that her teeth chattered, and his hands fell away to catch her shoulders.

He whirled her round in a sudden movement that made her head as well as her body spin. She moaned in protest as his mouth came down, cruel and punitive against her lips, parting them forcibly, demanding her surrender because he held her face between his two hands, his fingers crushing her cheekbones and allowing her no room to escape.

For one second her soft mouth trembled into an unwilling response and she groaned, then she made herself stand passively in his grip, while he descended from hot passion to a sensuous pleading, his lips coaxing unavailingly against hers.

When he finally released her she stumbled to the wash basin and leaned against it, fighting down waves of nausea. Ashley stared at her, then walked to the door and slammed it behind himself.

Weeping, Selina stumbled back to the couch and fell on it, her whole body limp with the aftermath of tension.

There had been so many similar scenes during their brief marriage. It had begun on the first night of the honeymoon. She had persuaded herself that because she loved Ashley she would be able to go through with all that marriage would mean, but on that first night she realised how much she had fooled herself. During their brief engagement he had kissed her passionately, and although she had been tense whenever he did, she had wanted that close warmth and been able to respond. When he came into her bedroom in his pyjamas on their wedding night he had not found a yielding, passionate bride but a demented, terrified animal, scratching and biting whenever he tried to come near her. He had been completely at a loss. He had begged her to explain, and her halting stammered words had tried to give him some glimpse of how she felt, but she had not felt able to tell him the whole truth, and so he had never really grasped what lay behind her instinctive dread of sex.

When the weeks went by and the situation was unresolved, Ashley had become angry. He tried to force her to see a doctor, but she refused. She could not even bear to talk about the ice barrier in her mind which came down whenever a man came too close.

At some point along the bitter road Ashley lost his patience. Selina woke up one night to find him in her bed, a little out of his mind with drink and repressed — passion. She fought him off and he slammed out of their house, saying he would find another woman as she was unwilling to sleep with him. That night Selina took an overdose, and he returned later to find her in a coma. She was dangerously ill for weeks, and when she came out of hospital it was to find that he had left her.

He visited the club where she was singing some weeks later with Clare Leslie in tow. A ravishing blonde, Clare was quite obviously infatuated with Ashley, and his ardent attentions made it plain that he was already her lover. Selina knew perfectly well that he had brought Clare there that night to make the situation clear to her. She saw her solicitor next day and divorce proceedings were set on foot.

Ashley arrived at her flat the morning the divorce papers were served on him, his face dangerous with rage and emotion.

When she tried to shut the door on him, he kicked it open and forced his way past her.

'What the hell does this mean?' he demanded, waving the papers at her.

Selina had drawn her negligee around her, facing him defiantly. 'What does it look like?'

'You're divorcing *me*?' The words were incredulous. 'I suppose you're planning on massive alimony!'

'I wouldn't touch a penny of your money,' she said, flushing deeply.

'Then why? In God's name why?' His face had changed as he looked at her, and with a shrinking dismay she recognised the look that came into his grey eyes. 'Selina ...' he had said hoarsely, his hand coming towards her. 'Don't do this!'

She had shrunk back against the wall, biting her lip.

'I'm sorry, Ashley, I should never have married you. It was a mistake.'

'A mistake!' Bitter fury made the words sting. 'You frigid little bitch!'

She had gone deathly pale at the insult, but bent her head, accepting it without retort.

After a pause he had said huskily, 'If it's Clare, you don't need to worry. I only wanted to make you jealous.'

She shook her head, her throat burning. 'It isn't Clare ...' Then she had looked up at him, sighing. 'It's me, Ashley. I'm sorry. It will be best to end our marriage quickly and cleanly. I'm the one to blame. If you prefer to divorce me, I'm willing, but I thought it would be easier if I did it this way ...'

'You don't love me,' he said harshly.

She hesitated for a moment, unwilling to lie yet knowing she had to if she were to end the barbed wire tangle of their lives.

Then she had said quietly, 'No, Ashley, I don't love you.'

He had sworn then, his voice savage. 'You married me for the money and then couldn't go through with it? Is that what I'm to believe? There's someone else? You're in love with another man? God, Selina, there has to be a reason.'

She weakly shook her head. 'Please, just go ...'

'Just go?' The words were spoken on a groan of physical pain. 'No explanations? No apologies? Just go?'

'I've said I'm sorry, and I mean it. I was very wrong to marry you. I regret it bitterly.'

'I'd like to kill you,' he had said quietly, almost as if he were talking to himself. 'But why should I waste any more of my life on a frigid little cheat who couldn't even go through with her own lies and pretences?' And he had walked out of the door and out of her life without another word. Until now ...

When her tears had subsided Selina sat staring at nothing for a long time, obsessed with unhappy memories. A sharp knock on the door made her sit up, wiping her face awkwardly with her hand.

'If you aren't out of there in two minutes I'm coming back in,' said Ashley.

She knew him well enough to know he meant it. Getting up, she washed briefly, expunging all traces of her tears, then she hurriedly changed into her usual clothes, hung her black dress carefully on its hanger, found her coat and was just about to walk towards the door when it was flung open.

He looked her up and down, his mouth twisting derisively. 'Back to normal,' he said. 'You should have been an actress, Selina. You have a natural ability to put a lie over.'

'I don't need your company,' she told him. 'Why don't you leave me alone?'

'My car is outside,' ignoring her protest. His hand clamped down on her arm, propelling her forward.

Short of struggling with him, she had no option but to obey. As she passed the office Freddie looked out, his brow creased in uneasy curiosity. From the way he glanced at Ashley, she saw that Freddie already knew that the report of Ashley's death in that air crash had been false. Freddie's monkey eyes were concerned as they met hers.

'You O.K., Princess?' he asked.

'She's perfectly all right,' Ashley told him abruptly.

He had never liked Freddie, blaming him for Selina's involvement in show business. The two men had been hostile from the start.

'I'd like to hear it from her,' said Freddie, bristling at once. He looked at Selina. 'You look as if you could do with a stiff drink. Come in and have one with me.'

Ashley's grip on her tightened. 'Come on,' he said, pushing her on along the passage. A few of the customers had appeared at the far end, laughing and shouting, and Freddie was forced to go towards them to shepherd them back to the front of the club. They were not allowed back here. While he was occupied with them Ashley hustled her out of the back door and into his long, silver-grey limousine.

She reluctantly sank into the front passenger seat, pulling her coat around her. He slid behind the wheel, slamming his door, and started the engine.

'I live . . .' she began, but he cut her off without looking at her, his voice crisp.

'I know where you live.'

The traffic had thinned now, of course. The theatre crowds had largely gone home. The pavements were sparsely populated, and the slow spitting rain had driven most of the late-night salesmen away into doorways, where they stamped their feet and blew on their fingers while they waited hopefully for someone to buy hot chestnuts or hot dogs. A few teenagers ran across the road, leaping like dervishes in their excitement. A policeman calmly strolling along his beat looked round at them in narrow-eyed observation, then walked on, seeing that they were only playing the fool. The road was blurred with the yellow reflections of street lamps on rainy tarmac.

'Your career is going well,' Ashley commented, his eyes intent on the road.

'Yes,' she agreed quietly. 'Thanks to Tom Kegan.' Her agent was a livewire of a man, always spawning new ideas, always on the lookout for some fresh avenue of approach. Selina had heard him called unscrupulous, but to her Tom had always been kind and rigidly honest. She had been with him now for three years and she had no complaints at all.

'If you always sing the way you did tonight you'll end up a star,' Ashley murmured drily. 'I could have lit a cigarette with the man sitting next to me. I thought he was going to burst into flame when you took off your gloves. Whose idea was that routine?' He glanced at her sideways, his eyes sardonic. 'Not yours, I bet.'

'Tom's,' she said briefly.

'Clever fellow. It's dynamite. The merest whisper of a strip tease ...'

'It is not strip tease!' she protested, flushing hotly.

'You certainly teased that audience. They were hoping for a lot more to come off ... which, of course, was the intention.'

Selina had disliked the act when Tom suggested it for the very same reason, but Tom had insisted and gradually she had grown accustomed to doing it, although she still had a habit of forgetting to take the gloves on with her so that she had an excuse for cutting that part of the routine. She wished desperately that she had forgotten tonight. She was deeply sorry Ashley had seen her sing. It was lucky she had had no advance warning of his presence in the audience or she might never have gone on at all.

He spun the car left into the road in which she lived and drew up outside the flats.

She unclipped her seat belt and put a hand on the door handle. 'Thank you for the lift,' she said quietly. 'Goodnight, Ashley.'

He made no reply, but his long, lean body uncoiled as he slid out of the driver's door and stood up, slamming the door behind him.

Selina got out, too, her heart beating in angry panic. Across the car she faced him, her colour high, her eyes wide and bright.

'We've got nothing to say to each other, Ashley. We never had. Please, don't start another row.'

'I thought you might like to give me a cup of coffee,' he drawled, watching her with his cold grey eyes. The wind blew back a thick strand of silvered black hair and he raked it down again with one hand.

She shivered. 'I'm sorry—I'm tired.'

His eyes narrowed menacingly. 'There's a lot of unfinished business between us, Selina. One day you've got to face that. If you thought I'd gone out of your life for good you were wrong. I don't give up anything without a struggle.'

'It's three years since our divorce,' she cried, her hands clenched at her sides. 'I'd forgotten you. Why bring it up again now?'

Suddenly dark red colour invaded his face and she saw his nostrils flare in temper. 'Forgotten me?' The words were flung back at her fiercely. 'You damned little liar!'

She walked hurriedly away across the pavement, hearing him behind her, his long strides covering twice as much ground. She longed to run, but dared not do so.

It would be an admission of some sort.

She reached the door of her flat with Ashley close behind her. By the time she had got her key into the lock he was at her side. She turned on him, her face pale.

'Will you go away and leave me alone?' Her voice throbbed with sick panic.

He stared back at her, his face filled with angry, confused emotion. 'How do you manage to make me feel like this?' he asked her in a low, thickened voice. 'You give me nothing, absolutely nothing, yet I can't stop wanting you.' His hand reached out, almost pleadingly, to touch her arm. 'Selina ...' He whispered her name hoarsely.

She took the chance to slide into the flat while he was off balance. As she began closing the door he leapt at it, kicking it open again. She shrank against the wall, shivering convulsively, her hands up to stop him touching her.

'No ... don't ... please ...' Her own voice sounded rough and unfamiliar in her ears.

Ashley stood totally still, watching her, for a moment. Then he made a sound of self-disgust and anger, turned on his heels and walked out of the door.

Selina crouched, tears on her cheeks, listening to the echo of his departing footsteps, then she closed the door and walked automatically to her bedroom.

CHAPTER TWO

HE was at the same table the following evening. Selina saw him as she turned to face the audience and her voice faltered briefly, not enough to alarm the others in the room, but sufficient to make Ashley's unsmiling mask lift in a brief sardonic smile. He was pleased to get that reaction, she realised, and pulling together every ounce of her will power she forced herself to go through her act as if he were not present. The enthusiastic applause which followed did not include him, she noted, with one quick, nervous look. He was leaning back in his seat, a glass of whisky in his hand, his frown giving him a menacing look.

He managed to evade the people backstage and follow her to her dressing-room, but she had taken the precaution of locking her door. His irritated rap made her stiffen on her dressing-table stool.

'Let me in, Selina, or I'll kick up such a racket that you'll regret it!' he threatened through the door.

She would have ignored him, but she was worried about Freddie's reaction. Freddie took things personally. He might actually try to throw Ashley out, and she knew very well that Ashley could do Freddie physical harm if he cared to try. He was a powerfully built man with a wild temper when he was aroused.

As she unlocked the door he came through it with a rush and halted to look at her.

Wearily, she asked, 'What do you want, Ashley?'

His silent look made her flush. She turned back to her dressing-table and sat down, continuing to cream off her stage make-up with hands which only trembled slightly.

'We've said all we have to say,' she told him, peeling away her false eyelashes.

'Why do you wear all that stuff?' he demanded, his hands thrust in his trouser pockets. 'You don't need it. You're lovely without any make-up at all.'

She felt her pulses quicken and hated herself for reacting. 'Please, Ashley,' she said quietly, 'just go, will you?'

'Have supper with me tonight,' he said casually.

His offhand tone did not convince her. She turned to look at him directly. 'There's no point,' she said patiently.

He stared at her, as if weighing up what to say next. 'I'm only over in England for a couple of months,' he said softly. 'Will it hurt you to have dinner with me?'

'It would be disastrous,' she said.

'Why?' His eyes watched her as if trying to read her face.

She shrugged. 'You know why.'

'I don't.'

'Of course you do!' she snapped, angry because the idea tempted her despite her realisation that it would only lead to a new turning of the screw of pain which had given her such hell before.

Ashley held up both hands. 'If I swear not to touch you? Won't that make you change your mind? A quiet, friendly meal together? How can that do any damage?'

It would feed her tormented passion for him, she thought resentfully, but he must never guess that.

'A meal in a public restaurant and straight back to your flat afterwards, alone in a taxi, if you prefer it,' he urged as she hesitated.

Her eyes probed his face anxiously. She wanted to say yes to him. The need to be with him was eating at her and she was too weak to refuse. 'All right,' she sighed.

His eyes lit triumphantly. 'I'll be waiting outside,' he said, leaving.

When Selina came out of the club she saw him leaning against his sleek silver limousine, watching for her, his dark hair ruffled by the night wind. She had a flashing vision of that dark head on a mountainside in the wreckage of a plane, and winced. At least he was still alive. She could bear anything but his total extinction.

He wore a dark lounge suit tonight, the jacket open to show the matching waistcoat across which a gold watch chain glittered. The watch had been his father's, she recalled, and he always wore it. As she walked towards him she could feel those cold eyes flicking over her possessively. He straightened as she joined him, his chin on a level with the top of her head. She looked up, flushing slightly at the look in his eyes.

His chin was slightly darker than usual, the faint trace of stubble visible at such close quarters. She felt a frightening desire to run her fingers over the rough skin.

'I thought we would try the new French place round the corner,' he said.

'That sounds very pleasant,' she said, trying to be cool and collected. It was hard with his physical presence dominating her every thought.

As if Ashley had realised why she was staring, his

hand rubbed along his chin. 'I forgot to shave before I came out,' he said. 'I'm sorry.'

'I hadn't noticed,' she lied.

His eyes teased her. 'No? I thought you were staring.' He lowered his face and briefly moved his chin against her soft cheek, making her body tingle with sudden awareness. The sensation was exciting without being alarming, and for once she did not jump away.

Without comment he handed her in to the car and got into the driving seat. They shot round the corner and parked at the far end of the narrow Mayfair street, outside a small white-shuttered restaurant.

When the proprietor took Selina's coat, Ashley's glance ran comprehensively over the pale cream dress she wore, a simple but well styled linen dress. His eyebrows flickered. 'A completely different girl,' he commented. 'I like you in the black silk, myself.'

She felt her cheeks burn. 'That's a stage outfit,' she said quickly.

His mouth quirked sardonically. 'Naturally,' he nodded blandly. 'You wouldn't be seen dead in it outside the club. It might give men the wrong idea.'

She looked down at the table, fiddling with the heavy silver knives and forks, pushing her glass away towards the centre.

There was a silence, then he said heavily, 'I'm sorry. That was uncalled for and I promise it won't happen again.'

He handed her a menu and leaned back, studying the one he held. She glanced down the items and sighed, mentally discarding most of them as too fattening. Ashley glanced at her over the top of his menu.

'Something wrong?'

She smiled faintly. 'Only that I must choose carefully or I'll put on pounds with all this delicious food.'

The grey eyes flickered over her again, one dark brow rising. 'I don't see why you need to worry. You're too thin, if anything.'

'I'm thin because I watch my diet,' she said.

The waiter appeared again, bowing, and Ashley glanced at her. 'What do you want?'

Selina ordered melon, steak and salad, and he grinned at her, saying to the waiter. 'Make that two. I might as well watch my diet, too!'

When he had given the wine waiter an order, he picked up the aperitif they had both chosen and sipped it, considering her from beneath his heavy eyelids. Nervously she tasted her own, licking her lips with the tip of her tongue as she grew more and more aware of his gaze.

At last she glanced at him, her chin lifted, but before he could say whatever was on his mind the waiter reapppeared with their first course and they began to eat.

The meal was simple, but beautifully cooked and presented, and she enjoyed it. She rarely ate out, preferring to save money and time by cooking at home, and she almost never drank wine. Ashley kept her glass refilled without her noticing it, and as the meal progressed her cheeks grew slightly flushed and her manner relaxed a great deal.

He kept the conversation light, discussing neutral subjects which could not bring them on to dangerous ground, and Selina found herself laughing as he told her a story about an American acquaintance who had had gold fillings in his teeth and been mugged in New York and robbed of them.

'Poor man,' she said, sobering. 'It couldn't have been funny at the time.'

'Far from it,' he agreed drily.

Their coffee arrived and he watched lazily as she added cream and sugar to his. 'Your memory is good,' he said softly, watching her add three lumps to his cup.

She felt herself flush betrayingly. 'I suppose it was just an instinct,' she said to cover herself.

'I remember you take it black without sugar,' Ashley drawled.

She dropped saccharine into her cup without replying. 'I gather your businesses are doing well,' she said into the little silence.

'I don't complain,' he agreed.

'How many hotels have you got now?'

'My accountants could tell you,' he said drily.

She sipped her coffee slowly, her eyes on a landscape hanging on the wall beside his head. A man walked past, halted, stared at her and then said pleasantly, 'Good evening, Selina. How are you?'

She looked up in surprise, then her face softened as she recognised a pianist who had sometimes accompanied her but who was now working as a solo act. 'Hallo, Don. How are things with you?'

'Fine,' he said in satisfaction. 'I've missed you, though.'

'I've missed you,' she said, aware in every nerve of Ashley listening to them. She did not need to look at him to test his reaction to this incident. She could feel his silent anger with every nerve end in her body. He had always been a jealous, possessive man.

Don glanced at Ashley and did a visible double-take as he met the steely glare of those dangerous grey eyes.

His throat closing on a swallow, he said uncertainly, 'Well, nice to see you, Selina ...' and moved off.

Selina glanced across the table. Ashley was still leaning back in his chair, his posture casual, but his face was black and fiery with temper.

'Who,' he enquired with visible control, 'was that?'

'A friend of mine,' she fenced.

'Clearly,' he snapped.

'He used to play the piano for me,' she added quietly.

'Why did he stop?'

She looked down at her half empty cup of coffee, shrugging without replying.

'Let me guess,' he sneered. 'He fell for you in a big way and you gave him the hands-off treatment.'

It was close to the truth, although Don had been too decent to need any 'hands-off' warnings. He had hinted once or twice, then quietly faded out of her life.

Ashley turned his head and beckoned the waiter. 'The bill,' he said calmly. Selina finished her coffee, refusing a second cup with a shake of the head. Ashley signed a cheque, handed it to the waiter and glanced at her. 'Shall we go?'

As they got into the car she realised that the perilously balanced truce they had attained for a while that evening had been wrecked by the encounter with Don. Ashley started the engine with a roar, his eyes brooding on the road. She became deeply aware of the muscled thigh close to her own, of the strong hands on the wheel, the physical tension emanating from him as he drove.

He parked outside her flat and leaned on the wheel, his chin resting on his hands, looking at her sideways. 'Thank you for the evening,' he said coolly.

'Thank you,' she said uncertainly. To cover her nervousness she glanced at her wristwatch. 'Goodness, it's well past midnight!'

'What happens at midnight? Do you change into a pumpkin?' he asked derisively.

'I usually go to bed,' she said, still trying to speak lightly.

'And always alone,' he said sardonically, his mouth twisting in a cruel smile.

Her temper flared. 'Would you rather I slept with someone?'

The grey eyes narrowed. 'We both know the question is purely hypothetical,' he drawled. 'The man hasn't been born who could get you into bed with him.' A pause. Then, 'Or has he?' And now his voice was slightly unsteady.

Selina opened the door. 'Goodnight, Ashley.'

She was half expecting him to follow her, but to her relief he stayed in the car, and as she entered the building she heard his engine roar and then the violent racing of the throttle as he zoomed away down the street at top speed.

He rang her next morning to ask her to have lunch with him, but she invented a polite excuse. She dared not allow it to become a habit—that was how she had got into the mess in the first place.

His voice was dry as he said, 'How about supper, then?'

'I'm sorry,' she said on a sigh.

'Lunch the next day?' his tone cooling rapidly.

'Ashley, I ...'

'Or supper? Or lunch the following day?' His voice sniped at her as he added, 'Name your own time and

place, Selina. Or tell me outright that you don't want
to see me.'

She took a shaky breath. 'I don't want to see you,'
she said unsteadily.

There was a crash which hurt her eardrums. Ashley
had hung up. Selina slowly replaced the receiver and
went into the sitting-room where she was busy polishing
every surface she could find. It helped to let off steam.
If she didn't keep busy she would break down.

For several days after that she heard and saw nothing
of Ashley, and decided that he had given up. She was
not even certain why he had wanted to see her again
in the first place. His manner indicated that he still
found her desirable, but whether anything remained
of the love he had once felt she could not guess. At
times she had even suspected that revenge was the
stronger motive at the back of his mind, a desire to hurt
her as she had hurt him. Love, as she knew from her
own experience, does not necessarily die because it is
mingled with hatred. At times she hated Ashley, at
others she knew she still loved him. Perhaps it was the
same for him. Perhaps hatred was more powerful than
love. She could not guess how it was with him.

Roger came to see her one morning as she finished
her breakfast. When she told him earlier that Ashley
had not been on the plane, and was alive, she had been
surprised by the genuine warmth of his expression of
relief. Roger had never been fond of Ashley, but then
it is never pleasant to hear of the violent death of anyone whom one has once known well.

When Selina admitted him to the flat she noticed
that he looked rather pale. He was a little taller than
herself, with similar colouring, his thin face faintly

weak in feature, his eyes restless, their colour more blue than green, his mouth soft and self-indulgent. He was always well dressed; he had good taste. Today he wore a young executive dark grey suit with a blue shirt and a quiet silk tie. His hair was lighter than her own, a lock of it falling down over his pale temples.

'So how did Ashley enjoy reading his own obit.?' he asked with a frivolous grin, sitting down to pour himself a cup of coffee from the pot on the breakfast table.

'He didn't say,' she murmured, seating herself opposite him and resuming her meal. 'Have you eaten? Would you like some toast and marmalade?'

'Mm, thanks,' he said, sliding a slice of bread into the toaster. He glanced at her. 'Has he altered much?'

She did not want to discuss Ashley, but she saw that Roger was determined to do so. 'He hasn't changed at all,' she said, although that was not strictly true. 'Why are you here, Roger? Why aren't you on your way to work? Is it money? A gambling debt? Tell me the truth. How bad is it this time?'

'Bad,' he said heavily, stirring his coffee. 'Selina, you don't think I would come to you again if I wasn't desperate?'

Her sigh hurt. 'I thought you were cured. I must be a fool. You told me you'd stopped gambling and I believed you. You haven't asked me for money for months ... why did you start again?'

'You don't know how I tried,' he said, his voice irritable. 'I never went near the tables for weeks, but one night I had to entertain a client and he insisted on going to a club. I had to play to keep him company.' His mouth twisted in a petulant, wry smile. 'He could afford to lose. I couldn't. I went on and on ...'

'You always do,' Selina said bitterly.

He hunched his shoulders and looked sullen. He could never bear to be blamed. He hated to admit he had done anything which could be criticised. He had the stubborn pride of the weak who when they fall, fall all the way, having no safety net to catch their folly.

'If you help me this time I swear ...' His voice began, but he could not inject any note of confidence into his oath, and the words tailed off miserably.

'Oh, Roger,' she sighed pityingly, looking at him with unhappy eyes. 'Why don't you ask for help from one of the societies who are organised to help gamblers? I've read about them somewhere. They understand your problem ...'

'I'm not sick,' he said furiously, 'Or mad. I can stop gambling whenever I like. I stopped for weeks—I told you. But now I'm on a winning streak. No one goes on losing for ever.'

'You do,' she said.

'If that's how you feel,' he said angrily, getting up, but he could not go because he had no one but her to go to, anyway.

He sat down again, burying his face in his hands. Through his fingers his shaking voice whispered, 'I've got to have the money, or I'm done for.'

'How much is it?' Selina asked despairingly. She only had four hundred pounds in her savings account. She had been putting it away steadily over the last few months in the hope of financing a trip to the United States when Tom got her a job out there. It would have to go. It would be a wrench, but what choice had she?

He hesitated. She looked at him with deep anxiety.

'Roger, how much?' Surely he could not owe more than a few hundred?

'Ten thousand pounds,' he whispered.

She went white. 'Ten thousand!' Her voice was incredulous. 'But ... I thought they never let you owe that sort of money?'

He bit his lip, his face as pale as her own. 'I ... borrowed from my firm.'

'Oh, God!' she moaned.

'I thought I'd win it back, but I went on losing. I borrowed three thousand, and they let me go on without saying anything ... then last night they said I had to pay by tomorrow or ...' He covered his face with shaking fingers again.

'You're mad!' she exclaimed. 'You're out of your mind. Where on earth would I get that sort of money?' She stared wildly at him, 'Roger, I've got four hundred pounds—that's all. And no bank would lend me a sum like ten thousand without some sort of assurance that I could pay it back.'

'If I haven't paid them by midnight tomorrow they'll kill me,' he told her feverishly. 'You know what happened last time, and that was only a few hundred pounds. This time I'll never walk again. They said so ...'

'Go to the police,' she said, her voice trembling. 'Tell them about the threat.'

His face broke into manic laughter. 'The police? Do you want to make certain I end up in the river? If I went near a police station they'd break me into tiny pieces.'

'Why do you do it? Why? I don't understand.' Selina

stared at him in bewildered misery. 'You know the consequences, yet you don't stop.'

'You've got to help me,' he begged, grasping her hands. 'You can't just let it happen!'

'How? What can I do?' she demanded in hopeless despair.

He took a deep breath. 'Ashley,' he said in a muffled voice.

She pulled her hands out of his grip and stood up abruptly. 'No! I can't. I won't.'

'He's my only chance,' Roger insisted. 'He wouldn't even miss the money, and he would do it for you ...'

She looked down at him with unwilling scorn. 'You know what you're saying, don't you?'

Roger flushed slowly, his eyes dropping.

'If I ask Ashley for the money he'll own me,' she said hoarsely.

Roger shifted uneasily. 'Sis ... Sis, I'm sorry. I wouldn't have asked you, but ... I'm terrified ... I couldn't take another beating up. I couldn't!'

The contempt left her face and her mouth softened. suddenly she no longer saw a well-dressed young man of twenty-two. She saw a shivering little boy in shabby clothes with dark bruises on his thin body and terror in his eyes, and she remembered a pallid, dying woman who begged her huskily, 'Take care of Roger ... promise you'll take care of Roger ...'

She moved round the table and bent to kiss the top of his head, her arm squeezing his shoulders. 'All right, Roger, I'll ask Ashley.'

He lifted his face to look at her miserably. 'You'll hate me for this, I suppose. I wouldn't ask if I wasn't desperate.' But already relief shone in the depths of his eyes and the air of strain had left his pale face.

When he had left for work Selina walked to the telephone and picked it up, biting her lower lip. It had to be done, yet it was physical torture to dial the number of Ashley's London office. While she waited for the ringing to stop her heart hammered furiously against her breastbone and she felt literally sick.

She was put through to his office and spoke to his secretary, who told her coldly that 'Mr Dent is in conference.'

'Will you tell Mr Dent that Selina wishes to speak with him?' she answered calmly, although her stomach was churning.

When the woman's voice reappeared her tone had altered. 'Mr Dent will speak to you now,' she said very politely.

Ashley's voice was abrupt. 'Well, Selina?'

'I . . . I would like to see you,' she had managed to say evenly, fighting down a sick apprehension.

There was a brief silence. She could almost hear him thinking. Then he asked slowly, 'When?'

'As soon as possible,' she said, her voice growing huskier with each syllable.

'Do you mean in my office? Or privately?' he asked.

'Wherever you like,' she said, knowing her tone was humble. She was in no position to make demands on him.

Again a silence. 'Is this business or social?' he asked in a silky tone which made her quiver.

'Business,' she whispered.

'I imagined it must be,' he said, and she winced at his stinging voice. 'How about now?'

'If—if it's convenient for you,' she stammered.

'Take a taxi,' he said and hung up.

She knew Ashley too well not to know how quick he was—he would already be making a very shrewd guess as to why she wanted to see him with such urgency when she had recently told him categorically that she did not even want to see him at all. Ashley knew about Roger's weakness. He had known during their marriage that she helped Roger with money. At the time it had been one of the bones of contention between them, but it had been lost in the more personal issues.

His offices were situated in a glass and concrete canyon of London. Selina had been there during their marriage but never since. Ashley's company owned a number of hotels, some of which ran casinos as an attraction for their guests, a fact which had angered her in the past.

She stood outside, nerving herself for the encounter. Then she walked through the electric doors into the foyer.

The lift seemed to take a million years. She stared at her own reflection in the small mirror on the wall. Her face was white, her green eyes as bright as fire.

Ashley's secretary stared at her appraisingly as she walked into the outer office. Maintaining a calm expression, Selina asked to see Ashley. The woman was in her late twenties, her short dark hair neatly styled. Her face was shrewd, unsmiling, competent. She depressed a key on her modern office console.

'Miss West to see you, Mr Dent.'

'Send her in,' Ashley's voice said, his dynamic energy undiminished by the static crackling on the line.

'Through the door behind you,' the secretary said calmly.

Selina opened the door, walked into the room beyond and closed the door behind her.

The office was large, a mushroom-carpeted oblong with windows all the way along the wall behind the desk. Ashley sat there, in a leather swivel chair, remotely authoritative in a dark lounge suit and immaculate blue-striped shirt.

He watched as Selina walked across the room towards him, his eyes travelling over her from head to foot, taking in the Russian-style coat she wore, with its huge dark fur collar, her flame-red hair and the nervous brightness of her green eyes.

He gestured to a chair facing him across the wide, polished desk. At his elbow stood a bank of telephones and a console like the one in the outer office.

She sat down, swallowing on a lump in her throat. She had rehearsed what she had to say, but suddenly the words had deserted her and she was too nervous to speak.

Ashley laid his hands flat on the desk and leaned back, watching her intently. 'Well?'

She sat up straight, unconscious of the fact that her terror showed in her pale face. Her carefully thought-out words had gone. Before her courage failed her altogether she plunged into a blunt statement of fact.

'I need to borrow ten thousand pounds,' she said rapidly. 'Will you help me?'

His eyes narrowed. He whistled softly under his breath, leaning back, his long fingers playing with a gold fountain pen. 'Ten thousand? A lot of money. Have you any collateral?'

'No,' she said huskily. 'But I swear I'd pay it back with the usual interest ... I'm really beginning to earn good money now. In a year or two I may have paid it back ...'

'What do you want it for?' he asked coolly.

She flushed deeply, bending her head. 'I ... can't tell you that, I'm afraid.'

'Roger?' he drawled.

Selina lifted her head to look at him without answering.

His upper lip moved in a cold sneer. 'Gambling again,' he murmured.

'Don't sneer at him,' she said, firing up. 'You make enough money out of boys like Roger.'

'People in glasshouses shouldn't throw stones,' he said bitingly. 'We both make our living in a less than admirable way. I run casinos. You sell your body.'

Colour ran flaming up her neck and face. Her eyes spat rage at him. 'You swine! I do nothing of the sort. I'm a singer!'

'Do you honestly think your voice is that special? It's your sexy body that brings the men flocking into the clubs, poor devils, dreaming of something you're too damned frigid ever to give them.'

She stood up angrily. 'Don't bother about the money —I'll get it somewhere else.'

'Where?' he smiled sardonically.

'I'll find someone to help me,' she said desperately.

The grey eyes narrowed. 'I didn't say you couldn't have it,' he drawled.

Selina halted, trembling, but knowing she really had nowhere else to turn, despite her brave words.

'Do you mean that?'

'Of course,' he shrugged. His eyes watched her. 'On the right collateral,' he added softly.

'I told you, I haven't got anything worth offering as collateral,' she said on a note of angry desperation, then she saw the way he was looking at her, his eyes running over her in an insolent, possessive fashion that brought her to a stricken silence.

'Oh, I wouldn't say that,' he drawled.

'No!' she breathed. 'You ... you really are a first-class bastard, aren't you?' Her eyes spat contempt at him.

Ashley shrugged. 'Take it or leave it. I'd say Roger wasn't worth the sacrifice, and knowing you, I realise it would be a considerable sacrifice, but also knowing you, and how you dote on that little rat of a brother, I think you'll consider my proposition.'

She ought to walk straight out of this over-opulent office without even speaking to him again, but the memory of Roger's desperation held her there, her eyes fixed on the carpet at her feet. Drily she whispered, 'Well, what is your proposition?'

'I give you the money,' he said softly. 'In exchange I get you back.'

'Marriage?' she whispered huskily. 'You want to get married again?'

He leaned back, his hands now thrust deep into his pockets. When she looked up at the hard, controlled face she could get no hint of what he was thinking.

'Not exactly,' he murmured.

She trembled, her hands clenching. 'I ... see.'

'I'm sure you do,' he said drily.

'And you think I'd agree to that ... that disgusting suggestion?'

'Up to you,' he said indifferently.

Selina struggled to control a desire to scream. 'I'll

see you dead first,' she said between clenched teeth.

His smile was derisive. 'I'm sure you'd like to.'

She turned and walked out of the office, letting the door slam behind her. The secretary stared after her, then glanced at the closed door with a curious expression.

When Selina got back to her flat Roger was waiting for her. He looked up eagerly as she let herself into the flat. 'Well?' he asked, his voice trembling.

She bit her lip, tears in her eyes. 'Roger, I ...'

'He wouldn't lend it to you?' Roger looked at her in horror. His face grew petulant, accusing. 'You were tactless with him. You weren't nice enough ... if you'd been nice to him he would have given you the money ... I know he would! Ashley was always crazy for you, even after your divorce. You could have twisted him round your little finger if you'd tried hard enough.'

She pressed her hands to her burning cheeks. 'Roger, he offered me the money, but ...'

'He did?' His eyes shone eagerly. 'Oh, thank God!'

'I couldn't take it,' she interrupted desperately.

He stared, without comprehension.

'He ... his ... terms were ... unacceptable,' she stammered.

'Oh, for God's sake!' Roger shouted, running his fingers through his hair. 'What did his terms matter? I'd do anything, anything, to get the money!'

'Even go to bed with a man you hate to have touch you?' she asked hoarsely.

Roger groaned, tears running down his face. 'Sis, I'm sorry ... I'm sorry ... I'm a rotten devil ... I know how ... I know what it does to you.' He pulled her close, her head against him, and stroked her hair. She yielded, weeping bitterly, and they stood in silence for a long while.

'Life's a swindle, isn't it?' Roger said at last, faintly. 'What have we ever got out of it, Sis? We were warped when we were kids, both of us, by that ... that ...'

'Don't even mention him,' she moaned, stopping his mouth with her hand.

'Have you ever told Ashley why you can't bear to be touched?' he asked, cuddling her.

She shook her head.

'Don't you think you should? He'd understand. Anyone would.'

She pulled away, sniffing like a little girl. 'No. I don't want him to know. I can't bear him to know.'

'Oh, God, what a mess,' Roger sighed weakly.

She looked at him, rubbing the back of her hand across her eyes. 'Roger, if you went away they wouldn't be able to find you. If I gave you my four hundred pounds you could take a plane to America.'

He grimaced. 'They'd find me sooner or later. And it would take too long to get a visa.'

'You could hide until you had one,' she suggested. 'Go to Scotland or into the country.'

He looked at her unhappily. 'Sis, they'd get you if I did.'

She stared incredulously. 'Me?'

'They threatened me with that already. They know I could never let them hurt you. If I vanished they'd come looking for you.' His eyes were sick. 'They said it would be a pity if your pretty face was ruined by acid.'

She shuddered. 'Roger!'

While they stared at each other in silence there was

a knock at the door. Roger started violently. He turned to stare at the door with petrified eyes.

Selina slowly opened it. Two men stood outside. They were very broad, very unassuming and their eyes were deadly. Roger gave a strangled moan.

One of them looked Selina up and down. 'What a pretty lady,' he told his friend. 'Be a pity if she got hurt, wouldn't it?'

His companion smiled quietly at Roger. 'We want our money, Mr West. Tonight. One way or another we mean to collect.'

Roger backed against the wall, shaking. His face was so white Selina thought he would pass out.

She lifted her chin. 'You will get your money,' she said with no perceptible trembling in her voice.

They looked back at her politely. 'When?' one asked.

'Will you wait while I make a phone call?' she asked.

They looked at each other, then shrugged. 'O.K.'

She picked up the telephone and dialled Ashley's number. To her relief he answered himself, his voice curt.

'This is Selina,' she whispered.

There was a little silence. Then he said, 'Yes?'

'I ... I accept your offer.'

He said nothing for a long moment, while she felt herself becoming colder and colder.

Then he said evenly, 'Very well, it's a deal.'

'W-when can I have it?'

'Now,' he said. 'Can you come here and get it?'

'Yes,' she whispered. 'Right away.'

She replaced the telephone and turned back to the two men, who gazed at her impassively.

'You'll have a cheque for the money later today.'

'We don't take cheques, lady,' he said sneeringly.

Her eyes were contemptuous. 'Not even from Ashley Dent?'

Their faces altered. 'Ashley Dent?' They exchanged another long look. One raised his brows and gave a low whistle. The other looked back at her. 'You a ... friend of Mr Dent's, lady?' A little smile touched his hard mouth.

'My sister is his wife,' Roger said, trying to impress them.

It did. They took a quick step backwards, staring at her. Then the taller of the two said, 'You never mentioned it before.' His face was suspicious.

Selina was weary. 'I have no wish to discuss my marriage,' she said coldly. 'Mr Dent's cheque will be with you tonight.' She began to close the door.

'No hard feelings, Mrs Dent,' one of them said, and now a shade of anxiety was in his voice.

She laughed ironically and closed the door. Roger wordlessly held out his arms, and she put her head on his shoulder, shivering. 'I'm sorry, Sis,' he said, his voice shaking. 'Sis, I'll see a doctor ... I'll get help ... I give you my word of honour, I'll break the habit somehow. Don't shake like that. Oh, God, what have I done to you?'

'I must go,' she said, straightening up. 'I said I would collect the cheque right away. Will you phone for a taxi for me?'

In the taxi she tried to force herself to be calm, but nerves were leaping all over her body and she had to clench her hands to make them stop shaking.

Ashley's secretary was not in the outer office. Selina

hesitated, wondering whether to knock on his door, when he opened it.

The grey eyes were enigmatic as they surveyed her. She hoped he could not see the tension she was experiencing, but something in the slow twist of his mouth made her suspect he knew exactly how she felt. Shutting his office door behind him, he gestured across the the room in which she stood. 'We'll go through here,' he drawled. 'There's a room where we can be undisturbed.'

She followed him reluctantly, not quite sure what he meant by that, and halted in panic as she found herself in what was clearly a private suite.

As if unaware of her reactions, Ashley sauntered towards a cocktail cabinet built into an alcove. Moving behind the bar, he selected a bottle and two glasses from the elaborate display inside the glass-fronted cabinet on the wall. Selina leaned against the door, breathing in a shallow, frightened fashion, one hand fumbling for the door handle while she watched him. Ignoring her, he poured out whisky into each glass adding soda generously to hers.

'You look as if you need a drink,' he commented drily, at last turning to face her. The sardonic eyes took in her taut attitude with mocking amusement. He held out her glass. 'There's no point in standing there as if you were going to bolt. You know you're going to stay.'

She looked at him with hatred. After a pause he put down her glass on the bar counter and leaned against it, sipped his own, the ice tinkling against the glass.

Slowly she moved across the room and picked up her glass. She swallowed the whisky with a grimace. She hated the taste, but Ashley was right: she needed it at this moment.

As the warmth of the spirit ran through her veins, giving her a false courage, she allowed her eyes to wander around the room. It was presumably a flat kept strictly for the convenience of the chairman when he needed somewhere very discreet to entertain. Selina could imagine what sort of guests he usually had up here, and her chin lifted aggressively as she took in the luxurious decor, with its cream and brown colours occasionally lit by a deliberate touch of gold. The carpet was cream, soft and deep underfoot. The floor-length curtains were striped chestnut and gold. The long sofa was covered in a silk print with a Chinese design in colours which matched the curtains. Pleated brown silk lamps stood on various surfaces. A stereophonic music deck took up half of one wall. It was a room meant for relaxation.

'Take your coat off,' Ashley invited, watching her. 'It's warm in here.'

'I'm—I'm not stopping long,' she said huskily.

His eyes pinned her against the bar. 'Take it off,' he demanded tightly.

She flushed, but obeyed. She had no choice. He had made the terms and she had accepted them. But she made a nervous plea for time, her voice trembling. 'I—promised I would take the cheque back to Roger straight away.'

'Not until I've inspected the collateral,' he came back as her voice died away.

It was no more than she had expected, but she could not help swallowing convulsively. 'Must it be now?' she asked weakly, her eyes wide and terrified.

He finished his drink and put it down with a crash which made her jump like a startled gazelle. Moving round the bar, he came towards her. 'On the sofa,' he said, his mouth biting out the words.

She backed shaking. 'Must you make it so brutally cheap?'

He had her by the elbows, smiling unpleasantly down into her face. 'Hardly cheap, my dear—ten thousand it a lot of money. You're a very expensive toy, what one might call a luxury item. I hope you're going to be worth it.'

'You ought to know,' she said bitterly.

His smile was cruel. 'Ah, but I'm hoping you've learnt something since we last met. That act of yours can't be all tease. Our marriage was a perpetual ice age, but even ice maidens thaw out eventually. You've had three years in which to gain experience. You must have learnt something.' The grey eyes narrowed watchfully on her face. 'There must have been men in those years.'

Selina looked down, her lashes dark against her cheek, unwilling to let him know how empty her life had been. 'Of course.'

He gave a harsh crack of laughter. 'You god-damned liar!'

Her head flung up. 'What?'

'I've had you watched twenty-four hours a day for the past three years,' he said derisively. 'The only man in your life is Roger.'

She was so astonished that for a moment she could only stare at him incredulously. Then she said, 'You—you had me watched? For three years? You must be mad!'

He thrust his hands into his pockets and moved away

from her. Over his shoulder he said coolly, 'I could afford it, and I was curious about you.'

'What did you expect to find out?' She tried to fathom his reasons for doing such a thing, but could not guess them.

'How you got the way you are,' he drawled, his back to her. 'Why you're locked in that frozen lake you call a body. You only have to walk across a room to have every man in the place dreaming about you. You're beautiful and sexy, yet you freeze every time anyone comes within touching distance. Let's just say I found you as hard to understand as a Chinese puzzle. I was looking for the key.'

'And did you find it?' she asked lightly, beginning to tremble a little. How much had he found out? What did he know?

He turned, his eyes hooded by the heavy lids. 'I think you know I didn't. You covered your tracks too well, didn't you, Selina?' The lids lifted and the grey eyes pierced her, probing her expression searchingly. 'What is it you're hiding? Why don't you tell me? You can trust me.'

She turned away, her lashes sweeping her pale cheeks once more. 'There's nothing to tell.'

She heard him draw a long, sharp breath, but he did not move. After a moment he said, 'Very well, let's go back a few years. Why did you marry me?'

'Please,' she said shakily. 'I don't want this sort of discussion. We've been through it all before, and it does no good.'

Ashley swore under his breath and she tensed, expecting some violent action, but he did not move. After another pause, as if he was turning over what to say next, he said slowly, 'Will you answer just one question frankly?'

'If I can,' she said cautiously.

His voice was expressionless. 'Is it sex you can't take? Or is it me personally?'

She gave an unguarded gasp of surprise, trembling a little. Before she had had a chance to consider the possible consequences of answering it she heard herself saying huskily, 'It—it isn't you personally.'

He moved then, his fingers firmly lifting her chin until she was forced to meet the grey eyes head-on. They were unreadable.

'How do you really feel about me, Selina?' he asked quietly.

She ran a nervous tongue-tip over her lips. 'Please!'

'Answer me,' he commanded shortly.

She could not hold the grey eyes. Her lids lowered as she said reluctantly, 'You know ... you frighten me ...'

'Why?' he pressed.

'Oh, please,' she twisted away from his grip, terrified of the insistent questions.

As if her flight suddenly snapped the control he was keeping over his temper, he caught her back, his hard fingers biting into her shoulders. Her alarmed, fluttering glance saw that the grey eyes were no longer unreadable. She recognised only too clearly the emotions which blazed in them and her body began to tremble in petrified response.

He stared down into her face, reading her reactions angrily. 'Is this how you're going to honour your bargain?' he asked savagely. 'I might have known better than to make a deal with a woman. If I were you, I'd remember that you haven't got that cheque yet, Selina.'

She stood still, looking back at him helplessly. A cruel, sardonic smile twisted his mouth. 'That's better,' he said. His hands drew her closer, moving down her body to press her in towards him. Involuntarily she clutched at him to steady herself, and an electric shock flashed through her at the feel of his warm, muscular chest under her palms. Through the thin silk of his shirt the heat of his body communicated itself to her skin and a pulsating sweetness began to throb deep inside her. She felt beads of perspiration break out on her temples. Swallowing, she tried to wriggle away, but his hands were unbreakable iron links against her hips.

He watched her intently. She could feel the insistent probing of the grey eyes even though she averted her face. She was past caring. All her energy was going into fighting her own rising desire. Her body seemed to be a channel through which a molten lava was flowing. The stillness of his body against hers was inflammatory. She had a terrible desire to touch him, to surrender herself to the clamour of her senses.

It was worse, she thought. Three years ago she had thought it could get no worse, but his absence had managed to feed the flame of her passion for him.

Ashley made a low stifled sound and at last she looked up at him, shivering. His face was darkly flushed. They stared at each other.

'We'll get married next week,' he said at last, his voice thick.

She stared in disbelief. 'But ... you said ...'

'I was curious to know how far you would go for that little rat of a brother,' he said furiously. 'I always meant to marry you, and this time I'm going to keep you.'

'But my career——' she began anxiously.

'Is over,' he said, his mouth biting out the words.

'I've got contracts ...'

'My lawyers will sort it out,' he snapped.

'Oh, but ...' Her eyes were panic-stricken. She had come here prepared for seduction, for humiliation, but it had never entered her head that he had intended anything so drastic as taking over her entire life like this.

'For God's sake, don't argue,' he said flatly. 'You want the ten thousand. Do as you're told. There's still time to pull out of the bargain, but make up your mind. Either you get the money and I get you, or the deal is off.'

Her eyes lifted to his face in anxious search. What exactly did he mean? That she was to give up all her freedom, abandon her career, become a prisoner?

'This wasn't what you suggested at first,' she pointed out. 'I thought ...'

'I know what you thought,' he said with a savage smile. His head bent suddenly and before she could move away his mouth was crushing hers in a fierce, punishing kiss which bruised her lips and made her wince, fighting against his strength. He drew back and stared at her insolently. 'That's what you came here to give me,' he said icily. The grey eyes ran down over her. 'Very tempting it is, too, but I want more than that for my ten thousand. I wouldn't find such a liaison sufficiently rewarding. I don't just want to sleep with you for a few nights. I want to own you.' His eyes insulted her. 'Well?'

Selina bent her head, sighing. 'Very well.'

CHAPTER THREE

A WEEK later they were in a plane flying to the Bahamas and Selina was trying to come to grips with the fact that once again she was Mrs Ashley Dent. It wasn't easy. She knew that one part of her brain did not want to believe it. Her first marriage to this man had been six months of unbearable torture. She must be mad to try again, especially when she knew it was all going to be the same again. She hadn't changed. As he slid the ring on to her finger earlier that day her whole body had been shaken with a sense of terror and total rejection. Ashley's quick, upward glance, those dark lashes flickering against his brown skin, had warned her that he felt the reaction she was unable to suppress. But he had merely leant forward to touch his mouth against hers, the brief kiss so light, so gentle that she had been able to suffer it without a cry of protest. Then Roger had hugged her, his face beaming. Roger, in his usual optimistic fashion, had managed somehow to convince himself that their remarriage was a matter of romance rather than business, as if his desperate need for that ten thousand pounds had no part in it at all.

Selina had been worried about leaving Roger. With his anxiety about money removed, she was afraid he would plunge straight back into wild gambling, fuelled by some secret belief that Ashley would bail him out again if he ran into trouble. Roger was an eternal optimist. She sighed, turning her head to look out of the window.

They were flying above cloud level. Below them she could see the milky white cloud layer floating like curdled goat's cheese, streaked with blue here and there, the whole illuminated by a shimmering brightness from the invisible sun. There was a dreamlike quality about it which she remembered from previous flights. The plane hardly seemed to move. They appeared to hang there while the clouds streamed slowly below them, moving on an ocean bed of blue sky.

A stewardess in a neat uniform paused beside their seats, bending a bright golden head in solicitous enquiry. 'Can I get you anything, Mr Dent?'

'Thank you, my wife will have some coffee,' Ashley said calmly. 'Black, laced with a finger of brandy. I'll have a whisky.'

The girl smiled. 'Yes, sir.' Her blue eyes surveyed him invitingly, admiring his casual, expensive lightweight suit, his open-necked silk shirt. Against the white silk his brown throat had a masculine virility which drew the eyes.

When the girl left, Selina looked down at her laced fingers nervously. They had not spoken since the flight began.

'Sure you don't want a magazine to read?' Ashley asked now, gesturing to a pile of them pushed into the receptacle on the back of the seat in front. 'I got you a selection.'

She moistened her lips with the tip of her tongue and his eyes fastened on the tiny movement.

'Nervous?'

She nodded, risking a glance at him.

'Of the flight?' His eyes were contemptuous. 'Or afterwards?

Selina flushed revealingly.

His right hand moved to touch hers lightly. 'I've told you, I'm in no hurry,' he said very softly. 'You can relax, Selina. At the end of the flight there's nothing to worry about ... just a quiet villa on a beach, lazy days and undisturbed nights.'

She looked at his face again, her eyes wide. Did he mean what he said? Or was he lulling her into a false state of confidence? Since that terrible day when she had gone to him for the cheque she had scarcely seen him. His lawyers had swung into efficient operation immediately to smooth out the problems their marriage would create, cancelling her singing engagements, somehow soothing Tom Kegan's irate, irritated reaction to the news, settling all her affairs without Selina having to do a thing. She meanwhile had fulfilled her agreement with Freddie and concentrated on Roger, who was euphoric with the threat of a beating up removed. He had sworn never to gamble again, but Selina had heard him make such a vow too often before to believe it. One evening Roger had had an appointment with Ashley, but she had scarcely seen her brother since then and so she had no idea what had been said between the two men.

The stewardess returned with their drinks and Selina reluctantly took a sip of her coffee, grimacing at the taste of the brandy.

'Drink it,' Ashley commanded. 'It will help your nerves.'

'You make me sound like a neurotic,' she said, half resentfully.

He shrugged. 'In one direction you are,' he pointed out.

She bit her lip, unable to deny it.

After a pause, she asked, 'Why did you want to see Roger two nights ago?'

'He didn't tell you?' Ashley demanded, his grey eyes probing her face.

She shook her head. 'Would I ask if he had?'

Ashley grimaced. 'I laid it on the line for him. No more gambling. I've put the word out that he's banned from the clubs. Most of the London casino owners are acquaintances of mine—they'll make Roger *persona non grata* in their places. If he shows his face they'll throw him out. He'll get no credit from anyone.'

Selina sighed. 'Thank you. I'm very relieved.' Her voice dropped into faint bitterness. 'A pity it didn't happen three years ago.'

'Once our marriage was dissolved it ceased to be my business what Roger did,' he said harshly. 'Why should I bother to stop him destroying his life?'

'He's weak,' she said. 'I think his gambling is a sickness. He needs help.'

'There are places which can offer him help,' Ashley nodded. 'I've given him an address. If he goes there he'll be helped.'

'And if he doesn't?'

'Look, Selina, you can't live your brother's life for him. If he wants to be cured of gambling that's one thing, but if he refuses to look for help then no one can help him. The only person who can help Roger is himself—don't kid yourself. I've shut a few doors on him, but there are ... shall we say less reputable gambling clubs? They may let him gamble, although they're unlikely to give him much credit.'

She nodded miserably. 'I realise that.'

He took a deep breath. 'Did he tell you that he'd actually embezzled from his firm? Part of the ten thousand had to be paid back before they found out or he would have lost his job. If he did that once, he can do it again, and next time I'm not bailing him out. It would be doing him no favours to let him think he can always get away with whatever he does. Sooner or later Roger has to face up to life without a feather bed to fall back on. You've always been there, protecting him from the consquences of what he did—you've got to let him stand on his own two feet now, otherwise he'll never grow up and be a man.'

She looked at him, her eyes tracing the hard bones of the dark face, the cool, steady eyes, the powerful jaw and level mouth.

'It's easy for you,' she said. 'You're strong. Roger isn't.'

'I've never had a sister prepared to sell herself body and soul to bail me out,' he said sardonically.

She flushed, looking away.

His hand moved to pick up one of hers, lifting it to his mouth, his lips cool and firm against her wrist and then her palm. 'That's what you've done, Selina,' he said softly. 'Sold yourself to me body and soul. You aren't going to cheat on our deal, are you?'

Her eyes widened, her hand shook in his grasp. She nervously moved her head. 'No,' she whispered.

'Good,' he said. 'Go to sleep. The brandy should have helped.'

When he laid her hand back on her knee, her eyes closed and she tried to relax. Slowly her weary brain ceased to revolve like a white mouse in an iron wheel and she fell asleep.

The villa was situated on the edge of a small town on the coast. Surrounded by luxuriant, well-kept gardens, it had a wicket gate which led down to a small private beach not overlooked by any other house. Behind the town the steep, forested, mist-shrouded summit of a hill rose sharply. The blue waters creamed on to the golden sands with a gentle swishing sound and the tropical trees in the garden were alive with small coloured birds.

Selina sat on the long colonnaded terrace staring out into the garden, a tall frosted glass in her hand, listening to the confused sounds of the birds and sea. They had been here for one night. She had been incredibly nervous as she ate dinner in the quiet, stone-floored dining-room, but as soon as she had eaten Ashley sent her to bed and he had not disturbed her that night.

Had he meant what he said? Had he no intention of trying to make love to her? But then why should he marry her? She did not think she could stand a prolonged cat-and-mouse game, knowing that one night, sooner or later, he would demand her surrender. The very prospect made her stomach muscles tighten intolerably.

A step on the terrace floor made her stiffen. She turned her head and found him lounging against the open french windows, a glass in his brown hand, watching her.

'Do you like the place?' he asked casually.

'It seems very pleasant,' she said cautiously.

He smiled without humour. 'Don't be too enthusiastic, will you?'

'I haven't seen enough of it yet,' she protested. 'Could we go into the town today?'

He shook his head. 'I don't think so.'

She frowned. 'Then what are we going to do?'

He shrugged. 'Laze around here in the house, on the garden lawns, on the beach ... I've been working hard lately. I need a complete rest.' His eyes skimmed her face penetratingly. 'So do you, by the look of you—you're as tight as a drum. You need to relax, let the world drift by. There's no need for us to do anything special. Just soak up the sun and forget everything else.'

'I haven't got much in the way of beach wear,' she said, her lower lip caught between her teeth.

'All you need is a bikini,' he said drily. 'Don't tell me you didn't pack one.' His grey eyes moved slowly, lingeringly, down her body. 'I like that dress, but there's too much of it. Go in and change into a bikini.'

Selina moved restlessly, twisting her glass between her fingers. 'I haven't finished my drink yet.'

'Then finish it and change later,' he said easily, joining her at the small table beside the terrace wall.

She put down her glass and stood up. 'It doesn't matter, I'll drink the rest later.'

His expression was mocking. 'Running away so soon, Selina?'

Her pulses quickened. 'You asked me to change,' she pointed out.

He smiled, and the lazy charm of his glance brought new colour flooding into her face. 'So I did,' he nodded softly.

She went back into the house. Her bedroom was a long, cool, shaded room at the land side of the villa. Trees grew close beside the tall windows. At night the white shutters were fastened over the windows to keep out the local insects, including the mosquito, which could wreak such havoc on white skins unused to the climate.

Selina looked through her clothes and found her bikini, hesitating for some time before with a sigh and a shrug she undressed and slid into it.

She considered herself nervously in the mirror. Tom Kegan had insisted on paying for her to make trips to a local beauty salon where she could have both sauna and sun lamp treatments. In consequence her skin was already a smooth golden brown which looked very good against the brief white bikini top, and she was quite used to wearing the bikini. Still she knew it would take a great deal of nerve to walk out on to the terrace again and face Ashley. She felt almost naked.

Why on earth did his gaze make her shake in that embarrassing way? Why could she nervelessly parade in front of someone like Tom Kegan or Freddie, yet feel sick and terrified at the thought of Ashley looking at her like this?

Remembering a white terry towelling robe she had packed, she looked for it quickly and slid into it. It was very short, just reaching the top of her bare brown thighs, but somehow it covered her sufficiently to allay her nervous dread of going out to join him again.

When she walked out on to the terrace it was an anticlimax to find it empty. Ashley's glass stood empty on the table next to her half-full one. There was no sign of him.

Sighing, she sat down and picked up her glass. She was just finishing the cool lemon and mint drink when Ashley came back. He was wearing black swimming trunks and carried a large towel over one arm.

'Very practical,' he mocked, his eyes on her bare thighs. 'You can use the robe after your swim, it will save using a towel. You'll dry in the sun anyway.' He produced a large bottle of sun tan lotion. 'See, I've thought of everything!'

'Are we going down to the beach?' Selina turned her head and gazed into the garden to avoid the necessity of looking at the muscled masculine body, her heart beating fast as he came closer.

'Yes,' he told her. 'Come on.' His hand touched her elbow, lifting her, and she obeyed without question, following him down the steps into the garden.

The violent colours of the bougainvillaeas flamed around them as they walked down the concrete path, the heat assaulting their eyes. The flowers were incredible: purple, crimson, orange, their long stamens curling like bright tongues coated with thick pollen, the fleshy leaves and petals soaking up the sunlight.

A fountain played in a shady patio, the crystal drops of water floating upward, irradiated with sunlight, then tumbling back down again to begin the same cycle once more. Within the white spray a rainbow of colour seemed to be centred as the sunlight split the jet of water into sparkling fractions of light.

Lush dark green trailing vines coiled around the palms. Ferns sprouted coolly in their shade. Within the little oasis a soft coolness was trapped during the day while beyond the trees the sun quivered and flamed on the golden sands. The flowers were exotic, unfamiliar, bewildering in their variety and brilliance. The hibiscus blared in scarlet trumpets beside the vivid yellow cassias, each centre holding a jewelled drop of dew in the morning, the residue of the dew collected earlier before the sun came up, still held in those flaming cups like precious wine.

They went out through the wicket gate on to the

sands. Ashley spread his towel and glanced at her. 'We can share it,' he suggested, tongue in cheek. 'Or you can lie in proud isolation, if you prefer,'

The towel was wide enough for two, yet she inwardly hesitated, knowing she dreaded being too close to him. Aloud she said, 'I really don't mind.'

He grinned, his eyes teasing. 'Liar.' He stretched himself out on the towel, donning dark glasses, his arms crossed behind his dark head.

Selina slowly sat down on the very edge, as far away from him as possible.

'Take off that damn robe,' he commanded.

Her fingers trembled as she undid the belt and slid her arms out of it. When she looked at him she could not tell whether he was watching her or not. His head was laid in such a way that he might just be staring up at the sky. The lenses of his glasses reflected the sun too brightly, turning them into mirrors which flashed back at her, defying her eyes.

She uncoiled, lying down on the edge of the towel. Suddenly his hand moved, making her jump, but his fingers offered her the bottle of sun tan lotion.

'Rub this into my back, will you?' he demanded casually, turning on to his stomach.

She took it reluctantly, staring at his lithe brown figure. Her tongue moistened her lips nervously.

Ashley appeared to be settling down to sleep, his dark head cradled on his folded arms, his face turned away from her to one side. The firm, strong back muscles were relaxed.

She slowly unscrewed the top of the bottle and tipped some of the lotion into the palm of her hand. Swallowing, she moved towards him on her knees and sat back on her heels beside him, nerving herself to touch him.

'Get on with it,' he said suddenly, without looking round.

Selina licked her lips nervously. Did he suspect what feelings he was arousing in her?

Moving her hand towards the small of his back, she let the lotion spill on to the brown skin in a cool trickle.

'Mmm ...' he murmured, 'that's good.'

She lowered her hand, braced for the impact of that first touch, but even so it made colour flare in her cheeks and she was certain he must hear and comprehend the thick intake of her breath as her palm first came into contact with his flesh.

His skin was warm and smooth beneath her hand. She began to smooth the lotion in, her fingertips and palm working in a circular motion upwards to his shoulder blades. Her eyes fastened on him, seeing the small dark hairs which roughened the surface of his skin, every pore and tiny line visible to her at such close quarters. She felt the muscle and sinew rippling under her hands and that involuntary muscular response set her pulses thudding.

By now she was unconscious of the quickening of her own breathing, or of the stilled, held breath of the man she was touching.

Suddenly he turned his head to face her, breaking her out of the spell which had held her. His features were oddly pale and strained, but his expression was masked by those mirror-like glasses and she was too distraught to notice him too closely.

'I'd better turn over,' he said lightly. 'You might as well finish the job.'

She hesitated while he slid over on to his back, her teeth holding her lower lip between their surfaces.

He seemed to fall back to sleep again, though, his arms flung out to either side, the palms open as if to absorb the sun.

After waiting a moment, torn between fear and a desire to go on touching him, she tipped the lotion out into her palm once more and began to massage his chest. He was breathing regularly, as if asleep, his face relaxed, the jawline tender, the mouth partly open, the cheekbones smoothed out of all angularity.

The vulnerability of that masculine body lying without movement under her hands was stimulating her buried desire for him. Her eyes flickered restlessly over the long, lean body. Even in repose he had a powerful sexuality. Her fingers smoothed down the thick dark hair on his chest, excited by the wiry roughness of it against her skin.

Her eye suddenly caught a flicker of movement behind the mirror lenses and she tensed, sitting back. Screwing the lid firmly back on the bottle, she lay down, her head turned away from him, struggling to regain an even rhythm of breathing.

The sun poured down over them like molten gold. The sound of the blue sea came rippling on to the sand. A few seabirds wheeled and cried above the foam-capped waves. Her trembling began to subside, her pulses eased. She took a few slow breaths, staring up at the blue canopy.

When Ashley moved her heart leapt. She turned, her eyes wide and apprehensive. He had the bottle in his hands. She watched without speaking as he unscrewed the bottle and tilted it over his cupped hand. Thick, creamy lotion poured out.

She sat up, protesting hoarsely, 'There's no need ... I ...'

Wordlessly he pushed her back against the towel and crouched beside her. The mirror lenses hid his eyes. She dared make no further protest, though, as he began to smooth the cool lotion on to the pale golden skin of her midriff.

Her heart was beating so wildly she knew he must hear it. She held herself stiffly, unable to relax, watching him with the mute anxiety of a trapped animal.

Slowly the long fingers slid up to her shoulders, softly moulding her muscles, finding the hollows and defining the shape of her throat, their touch caressing. When they wandered down towards the swift rise and fall of her breasts she sat up again, huskily saying, 'No!'

Again that imperative hand pushed her back while the free one slid beneath her back. Panic was fluttering in her throat like a wild bird. She struggled to get up again, but his hand held her down while that other intrusive hand deftly unhooked her bikini top.

Her eyes closed helplessly. 'No,' she moaned, her head moving from side to side.

He knelt over her, anchoring her with his knees, while he freed her breasts from the bikini cups, his fingers lightly caressing.

There was a pause, during which her drumming pulses made it impossible for her to guess what he was doing, then she felt the coolness of the lotion smoothing into her nipples, and a long groan forced itself out of her, despite her attempts to stifle any response.

His hands ceased their movements, the palms cup-

ping her breasts in a warm caress. She could feel him
watching her. Her lids remained shut, only her lashes
stirring against her cheek to betray her awareness of
what he was doing.

One of his thumbs moved suddenly, stroking across
her nipple, and surprised another sharp sound of
pleasure out of her. Hot-cheeked, shaking, she opened
her eyes and dared to look at him. The lenses totally
hid his expression. His mouth was hard and firm below the arrogance of his long nose. Helplessly she stared
at that mouth, murmuring thickly, 'Please ... I ...
can't we swim now?'

His lips twisted sardonically, but he stood up, watching her without comment as she hastily re-hooked her
top and joined him, her head averted.

'Race you into the water,' he said suddenly, turning
on his heel. Selina followed him down the hot sand into the water, splashing through the shallows. Ashley
struck out strongly, but she floated on her back, staring
up at the incredibly blue sky, obsessed with what had
just happened on the beach. Suddenly strong hands
pulled her down. She screamed, half laughing, unafraid out here in the water. His naked body wound
around hers, they rose again into the sunlight, her wet
hands involuntarily clutching at him, her long wet
hair flicking across his smiling mouth.

Their faces were very close. The grey eyes laughed
into hers, full of friendly teasing. 'You were a tempting
target, dreaming along on the top of the water ... suppose I were a shark? I'd pull you down into my lair and
gobble you up bit by bit.'

'I dare say you would,' she retorted. 'I always knew
you reminded me of something ... a streamlined, ex-
clusive shark!'

He rubbed his salty wet cheek against hers, his hair slicked close to his head. As he turned his face their mouths brushed softly against each other. Suddenly the blue sky and the blue sea stood still. Her arms tightened around his neck; his hands tightened on her naked body. Their mouths met with the explosive rush of a tidal wave. Her eyes closed tight, Selina clung to him, her lips opening to his. The kiss deepened and took fire. Her heart was racing.

Then she was free again, rolling with the foam-capped wave, and the streak of his powerful body cutting through the water ahead of her was the only reminder of what had just happened.

She waded up the beach, shivering slightly. Ashley was wrapping himself in the towel, a few grains of yellow sand clinging to his wet hair.

'Lunch now,' he said, without looking at her.

She picked up her robe and slid into it. Had that moment of utter freedom out in the sea been a dream? For the first time in her life she had given in to the sexual urges she dreaded, and it had been as exhilarating as riding the white surf.

The maid, Joanna, lived in a small flat above the garage next to the villa with her husband, Amos, and her two children, Abram and Sara, two tiny black mites with eyes as big as lollipops and grins as wide as melons.

Amos took care of the garden and the various odd jobs around the villa, while Joanna saw to the cleaning and cooking. When the villa was not in use they were free to do as they pleased so long as the place was kept in constant readiness for occupation.

Joanna served the meal cheerfully, singing as she bustled to and fro with dishes. If she was curious about the fact that they did not share a bedroom she had given no indication of it.

Selina was surprised to find herself extremely hungry. The hours in the sun, followed by that short swim, had given her an appetite. She devoured the melon, steak and salad with appreciation, bringing a smile of pleasure from Joanna and wry comment from Ashley.

After lunch, at his suggestion, they both took a siesta on their beds since the heat of the afternoon made the garden somewhat uncomfortable for a few hours.

Selina changed into a brief yellow sun dress with thin straps over the shoulders. She lay down on her bed and found it easy to drift into another light doze. The stillness of the garden outside her window was conducive to relaxation.

Someone entering her room made her blink, her eyes flying open. Ashley stood at the side of the bed, watching her with most imperturbable expression. He had changed too, and was wearing light slacks and a cream T-shirt.

'What do you want?' Her tone held alarm and at once his mouth turned down at the corners.

'You said you'd like to go into town,' he reminded her. 'I thought we could combine it with a shopping expedition. You need some beach gear, don't you? And so do I.'

She flushed, swinging her legs off the bed. 'Oh! Thank you. Yes, I would like that.' She began to look for her sandals, but he was on his knees in front of her already, sliding the sandals on her bare feet, his hands deft as he did up the buckles.

'Your legs are incredibly long and beautiful,' he said

in an almost neutral tone. His fingers slid lingeringly over her ankles and moved up her calves. 'You're going to get very brown while you're here. How did you get this tan in London?'

'Sun lamp,' she said huskily. It was impossible to make light conversation if he insisted on touching her in that sensuous, distracting fashion, yet she dared make no protest.

He stood up, and she rose too, which proved a mistake, since it brought them far too close for comfort. His eyes observed the expressions flitting across her mobile face, one dark brow lifting in sardonic comment.

'You're going to have to get used to seeing me in your bedroom,' he said in a conversational tone. 'I'm going to be around all the time. You needn't jump like a frightened rabbit every time I come near you, though. I've no intention of raping you.'

Selina flushed hotly, her lashes lying dark against her sunwarmed cheek. 'I—didn't expect ...'

'Oh, yes, you did,' he drawled mockingly. 'You've been expecting it ever since we got here. I thought I explained clearly enough ... I'm in no hurry to consummate our marriage. You can relax. I don't want an enforced surrender. Sacrificial relationships have never attracted me.'

She stared at him, her eyes wide in puzzled enquiry. 'But ... our bargain ...'

'I didn't say I never intended to sleep with you,' he said coolly. 'Just that I'll do it in my own good time. There's no rush.'

She looked at him through her lashes, ludicrously irritated by his composure. Although she was terrified of the moment when he would demand that she honour their bargain, she was piqued that he should be so casual about it. What had happened to the old fire and urgency with which he used to besiege her? Was it possible that it had vanished?

Softly, her tone testing out his reaction, she said, 'You've kept your side of the bargain. I have no intention of refusing to keep mine, Ashley. You have the right to take what you paid for any time you want to.'

She was astonished by the look of fury which appeared on his face. The lines of his jaw tightened. The steel grey eyes were like bits of ice as he stared down at her. 'Do you think I don't know that? But I remember what it was like before. I've no intention of forcing a terrified woman to accept my lovemaking.'

She should have left the matter there, but contrarily her pride was pricked by the biting tone of his voice and the coldness in the grey eyes.

'Perhaps it will be different here,' she said softly, her eyes widening in bright green invitation.

She heard his breath catch and saw the coldness fade out of his hard face. His hands caught her by the waist, drawing her towards him. As the hard masculinity touched her she knew that this was what she had wanted ever since those moments on the beach. Her heart quickened, drowning her qualms. She let her hands slide round his neck to knot themselves into the salt-stiffened strands of his black hair, her body melting against him. Ashley stared down incredulously into the uplifted face, his eyes probing hers. As he did not move any nearer she stood on tiptoe, her mouth lightly brushing his, and with triumph heard the deep groan which issued against her warm lips.

Then his mouth came down hungrily, parting her lips, and the stark impact of his desire for her swept her away like a straw on flood water, his hands moving sensuously over her back to press her closer. Boneless in surrender, she arched herself towards him, her eyes shut tight in an abandon which had never touched her before. The first bruising demand of his mouth slowly softened to a sensuous coaxing, bringing her shuddering to a realisation of the reality of her feelings. She knew she did not want this to stop. She wanted him to go on kissing her, touching her like this. She had wanted it with increasing desperation for days. While her body let him mould her between hard, desiring hands her mind sought feverishly for the moment when her totally unexpected reactions had begun, and found the answer at that moment when she had read of his death in the air crash.

Wasn't that the moment when she had realised that her love for him was stronger than her fear of the demands of his body? She had not had time to consider that reaction before he had appeared at the club that night, but now she knew that part of her grief for his death had been the dull realisation that she had never shown him how much she loved him.

Her mind came back from its exploration of her own feelings to a leap of awareness of his, finding herself being lowered to the bed by his demanding hands.

His mouth covered hers again, one hand moving down to touch her breast in a warm, caressing movement which made her gasp under his kiss.

When the hand slid down under her dress, moving against her, the dark hair on the back of it roughly caressing her skin, she gave a sharp, panic-stricken cry, pulling away from him.

'Don't fight me, darling,' he said hoarsely, holding her still with the weight of his body. 'Don't be frightened ...'

'Let me go!' she exclaimed fiercely, struggling to escape, the hard power of his body making her old fear rise up redoubled.

He pulled her head round, staring down into her eyes, his face cruel. 'You can't do this to me,' he said thickly. 'You aroused me deliberately, you little bitch!'

'I'm sorry,' she quavered, tears rising to her eyes at the impossibility of explaining the confusion of her feelings; the struggle between love and fear exhausting her.

'Sorry?' His voice was savage. In a sudden vicious movement his hand slapped across her face, sending her head spinning.

Still dazed, Selina broke free briefly, only to have him pull her back against him, his body deliberately brutal as he used his superior strength to force her to lie still. His hands took hold of her dress, ripping the front of it, and she gave a short, choked scream which died under the crushing savagery of his mouth. He kissed her endlessly, his mouth exploring the softness of hers without compunction while his hands moved over her ruthlessly, making her body yield to his touch as helplessly as her mouth.

Then suddenly he stopped, turning his face into her neck with a harsh groan. 'Oh, God, Selina, what the hell am I doing to you? Why in heaven's name did you incite me to lose my head?' He lifted his face, his nostrils flaring white against the dark flush of his cheeks.

Wet-eyed, pale, shivering, she forced herself to meet the accusing grey eyes.

'You made me do that,' he said heavily. 'Admit it or not, you made me do it.'

'I admit it,' she said in a low, shamed tone. 'I'm sorry . . .'

He stared at her, probing her eyes. The tears began to fall faster, running down her cheeks in a stream. Ashley sat up and pulled her up against him, his hand lifting her hair, winnowing it through his fingers.

'All right,' he said gently, 'there's no need to weep. God knows why you did it, but there's no harm done.'

'I'm sorry,' she whispered, turning her face into his chest, hearing the leap of his heart as her cheek rested against him. 'I wish I could explain.'

'Selina, I know,' he said flatly. 'I know about your stepfather.'

CHAPTER FOUR

ALL the colour left Selina's face. White and shuddering, she faced him, her widening eyes trying desperately to read the expression in his direct gaze. His face told her nothing of his reactions. A cool, unyielding mask, it hid his thoughts entirely. She thought feverishly, guessing how he had heard the truth, yet recoiling from what he would say next.

'That night I had my chat with Roger,' he said carefully, 'I did what I should have done years ago—I asked him about your life before we met. He was reluctant to talk, which made it obvious that there was something I ought to know.'

She drew a long hard breath, her hands linked together at her waist to stop them trembling too much. 'You ... you didn't threaten Roger, did you?'

The grey eyes flickered. 'I didn't have to, but I would have choked the life out of him if it was necessary,' he said, and behind the level tone lay a seething violence which startled her. He was silent for a moment, then added, 'No, I just made it clear to your dear brother that if he wanted any further help from me he had to co-operate.' He grimaced. 'To do him justice, he seemed to understand that it was in your best interests for me to know the whole truth.'

'The ... whole truth?' Her voice was rough.

Ashley's face became a cool mask again. 'He told me the bare bones of the story. The rest of the details I filled in with the help of a newspaper file.'

A hard spot of crimson had sprung up in the centre of her white cheeks. She drew away from his protective arm and sat down on the edge of the bed suddenly, as if her legs could no longer support her, her head bent like a little girl's, her red-gold hair falling down over her bare neck in a glittering swathe.

'So you know,' she whispered in a thread-like voice. She felt very tired, as if she had run a long hard race and was now free to collapse at the tape.

'Your stepfather was a brutal animal, who used to beat up both Roger and yourself whenever he got drunk,' he said quietly, his eyes fixed on the bright, bent head. 'He beat your mother up, too, and she was petrified of him. Roger told me you used to hear her crying in her bedroom.'

Her body shook as if with silent weeping. 'Yes,' she whispered. 'It was ...' The words stopped abruptly and she swallowed on a harsh sob.

'His treatment of her made her ill,' Ashley went on carefully. 'She started to stay in bed all day.'

'She got thinner and thinner,' Selina whispered, as if to herself. 'She was like a fading ghost.'

Ashley pushed his hands into his pockets, his mouth grim. Very cautiously he went on, 'Then one night ...'

'No!' she moaned, shaking her head. 'Don't!'

'We have to talk about it,' he said roughly, his eyes filled with pity as he watched her.

She relapsed into silence then, her slender body shuddering with shock.

'You were sixteen,' he said quickly. 'He came home drunker than usual, and after beating you up until you were semi-conscious he tried to rape you.'

Selina gave a low moan of horror and disgust, wrapping her arms around her body, her head still bent. She was shaking so hard her teeth began to chatter.

Ashley pulled the white coverlet from the bed and wrapped it around her, registering without comment the violent shock which hit her body as his arms touched her.

Walking back across the room, he drew out a wicker chair and sat down in it facing her. 'Now that I know, wouldn't you like to talk about it?'

She shook her head rapidly.

'Selina, you have to talk. This has been festering in your mind for years. I want to cut it out—a quick, clean operation. Tell me everything, particularly the parts you don't want to remember.'

'I can't,' she said huskily.

'You can if you try,' he pleaded. 'You've got to tell someone, to get rid of the buried memories you've been carrying around for far too long.'

'I don't want *you* to know,' she wailed.

'Me especially?' he asked intently, watching her with narrowed eyes.

She nodded dumbly.

'Why not, Selina?'

Her eyes lifted at the tone of his voice, and his face tightened at her expression.

'You can't imagine I would blame you?' he asked gently. 'For the savage act of a drunken brute?'

'The court seemed to think I was to blame,' she said, her voice catching. 'The defence counsel kept hinting that I'd wanted ...' She stopped again, shuddering.

His face darkened. 'I know the way they work,' he said. 'Courts often seem to think the woman is as much to blame as the man.'

'It was ... like being attacked again ... this time in public with a room full of people looking on,' she stammered.

He half moved as if to come over to her, then sank back, his hands clenching at his side impotently. 'I'm not going to do that to you, Selina,' he said gently. 'I'm just going to listen while you tell me about it. I'm on your side.'

She took a deep breath. 'Roger was asleep when ... when he ... came home. He came into my room, but I ran away from him. I thought he meant to beat me up again. I ran downstairs ... he came after me and kept hitting me and hitting me. He knocked me to the floor. I was half dazed. I lay there, not even realising what was going on, until I came to and found him touching me.' Her body shook violently again, her teeth chattering. 'I screamed. I was lucky—the man next door had just got home from night work, and he knocked at the door. He—my stepfather swore at him and told him to go away, but I went on screaming, so the man next door broke the window and climbed in.'

Ashley moved across the room tensely, pulling her close to his chest, one hand moving through her hair. 'All right ... it's all right, Selina.'

As if she could not stop now she had started, she went on, 'I couldn't have stopped him, he was too strong. He was hurting me in that horrible way and I couldn't move ...'

Ashley's arm tightened. His face was pale. 'But he never actually ...'

She interrupted. 'No, he was stopped in time, but by then I felt just as unclean as if he had ... and as guilty ... especially after the trial. When it was all over my mother died. Roger and I changed our name and Freddie found us a cheap lodging. We had to hide or the authorities would have taken Roger away from me. I worked in the club to earn money to keep Roger. I'd promised my mother ...'

'And your stepfather died in prison?'

'Yes,' she said briefly. 'He caught pneumonia, they said.'

His hand stroked her hair softly. 'No wonder you found sex so terrifying. Why in God's name didn't you tell me the truth?'

'I couldn't bear the idea of you knowing,' she said huskily. 'I wanted to forget it ever happened.'

'But you couldn't,' he said flatly. 'Why did you marry me, Selina?'

'I ... I loved you,' she said wistfully. 'That first time we met in the club you weren't like so many of the men who tried to date me. Your hands didn't wander. You were gentle and ... and controlled.'

He grimaced. 'Controlled? That impression soon faded, didn't it?'

She flushed. 'It was my fault. You got angry with me. I'd let myself drift into a daydream.'

'And on our wedding night the truth blew up in my unguarded face,' he said with a dryness he could not disguise.

'I tried to stop myself fighting you, but every time you came near me my reaction was automatic.'

'And understandable,' he murmured. 'You were mentally and physically scarred by what happened, first on that night, and later in the court. If only you'd told me this years ago, we would have both been saved a lot of grief.'

Selina nodded wearily. 'It was very wrong of me to marry you. I knew I was frightened of the physical side of marriage, but I let myself believe it would be all right with you. I was afraid that if you knew about what had happened you'd feel differently about me. In court people stared at me ...' She closed her eyes, fighting down a wave of sickness. 'For years I used to dream about those curious, knowing eyes ... endless nightmares almost as bad as the others.'

'Do you still have nightmares?' he asked.

'Only occasionally,' she said faintly.

Ashley was silent for a while. 'Now that I do know, how do you feel?'

She lifted her face, her eyes wide and filling with astonishment. 'It ... isn't as bad as I'd expected.'

He smiled at her. 'I told you it wouldn't be. Nothing ever is.'

Her lashes fell and she smiled slightly. 'You've been very kind, Ashley. Very understanding.'

'Did you really think it would make any difference to how I thought about you?' he asked huskily.

'I was afraid it would,' she admitted. 'It might have been at the back of your mind all the time ... an unspoken suspicion about me, an uneasiness.'

He lifted her chin with tender fingers so that her eyes met his, and she saw a smile in the depths of his grey eyes.

'There's nothing at the back of my mind but a wish to see you become a whole woman,' he said softly. 'You were frozen between childhood and womanhood by a brutal act. You've got to take that final step, Selina. Outwardly you're a shatteringly lovely woman, but inside your head, as we both know, you're still a frightened child. We're going to help you take that step, but gradually, bit by bit, as naturally as it would have happened in your adolescence.'

She turned her face confidingly into his hand, rubbing her cheek against his palm. 'I want to ...' she whispered shyly.

Ashley's breath caught and a passionate darkness grew in his eyes. But he moved away from her. 'Give yourself time. Let the sediment settle.'

A rattle at the door handle made them both jump. Ashley gave her a grin. 'Joanna,' he whispered. 'Wondering what the hell we're doing in here with the door locked at this time of day!'

Crimson stained Selina's face. 'Oh, dear, what on earth must she think?'

'I can imagine,' he said mockingly. 'Come on, we'll go and do that shopping. We can both do with a walk.' His hand was extended to her and unfalteringly she placed her fingers on his palm.

They walked down to the town centre along narrow lanes, passing donkeys and busy workmen, pausing once to admire a small garden set with white waxen datura bells, their branches interlocking and making a thick virginal bower around the thatched house. The hills behind the town were darkening around the rims as evening settled down. A cooler breeze blew in across the sea. The heat slowly sank as the sun sank into the horizon.

'It's so unreal,' Selina murmured, gazing up into the forested hillsides. 'Too much of everything. The sky is too blue, the sea too calm, the flowers too thick and bright. It's like a mad fairy world where things grow like the magic beanstalk overnight.'

'Perhaps you need a little dreamy unreality,' Ashley said. 'A space to breathe in for a while.'

'Perhaps we all do,' she agreed. 'Even you, Ashley.'

'Oh, I know what I want,' he said coolly.

She looked at him in wary curiosity. 'What's that?'

He grinned at her, his jawline unyielding. 'I'll tell you one day when I've got it.'

'Not before?'

'Certainly not before,' he said. 'Don't you know the old saying ... tell a wish, lose a wish?'

'No, I never heard that before.'

He laughed. 'Hardly surprising. I just made it up.'

'I remember that when you blow out your birthday cake candles you mustn't tell anyone what you wish for as you do it,' she said thoughtfully.

'Same thing,' he agreed. 'It's unlucky.'

They found a modern shop which sold beach gear of all sorts and Selina wandered around it, buying straw beach sandals, a gaudy green beach hat with a wide brim, a large capacious straw beach bag lined with plastic to protect it against spillages. Ashley joined her with a package as she left the shop, and she looked at it curiously. 'What's that?'

'A present,' he said.

'For me?' Her eyes widened.

He slid it into her beach bag. 'Open it later.'

They sat down at a table under a striped umbrella and ordered a long, cool glass of iced orange juice sweetened with a concoction of more tropical fruits.

A young man in jeans and a gaudy T-shirt strolled past, stopped, stared at Selina closely and after a moment came up with a polite smile.

'I know it's an old line, but don't I know you?'

She regarded him with unconscious hauteur. 'I don't think we've met,' she said coolly.

He looked hard at her, smiled briefly at Ashley and said, 'I'm sorry, but I think we have ... I'm on holiday here from London. You sound English. I'm sure London is where I've seen you before.'

Ashley had been guardedly indifferent for the first few moments, but the young man's persistence had begun to annoy him.

'My wife says she doesn't know you,' he said firmly. 'That should be good enough for you.' He stood up, giving her his hand. 'We must get back, Selina.'

'Selina!' The young man's voice rose with excitement. 'That's it ... you're Roger's sister!'

She turned back, her face changing. 'You know my brother?'

'I work in the same office,' he said, laughing. He was

about the same age as herself, a tall, fair healthy-looking young man, with a smooth tan and direct, friendly eyes.

'How extraordinary,' she said.

'Small world, isn't it?' His grin included Ashley, who did not return the friendliness. 'You're on holiday too, I take it?' He glanced at Ashley again with the uncertainty of a strange dog in a house where they don't like dogs. 'I suppose you wouldn't have a drink with me? I've been here a week and I hardly know a soul. This isn't the height of the season, and most of the people at my hotel are middle-aged. I'm dying for a chat with a friendly soul.'

Selina glanced at Ashley enquiringly. His face was set like polished teak, his eyes cold. 'Sorry,' he said bluntly, 'we're in a hurry to get home.' His hand insistently pulled at Selina's fingers and she felt compelled to move away with him.

'Goodbye,' she said, with a smile at the young stranger. 'Nice to have met you.'

'Perhaps we could meet again,' he said eagerly. 'when you aren't in such a hurry. I'm staying at the Lorelei Hotel. My name is Phil Webster.' He followed them, his eyes pleading with her. 'How about tomorrow? Just for a drink? As I know Roger?'

'We'll ring you,' she said gently.

He stood still, watching them walk away. Selina turned back to Ashley accusingly.

'You weren't very nice to him. I thought he was genuine. He did know Roger—it wasn't just a line.'

'I'm here to enjoy myself,' Ashley said curtly, 'not to make idle chit-chat with a homesick young Lothario who hasn't the manners to realise when he's not wanted.'

She flushed angrily. 'That's unfair! He did recognise me.'

'He took one look at that desirable body of yours and he was sunk,' Ashley said tightly. 'It was just pure luck for him that he actually did know Roger. He was hoping for an excuse to get into conversation with us long before he found out who you were.'

'You have got a nasty mind!'

'I have!' He laughed angrily. 'I think we can assume my cure is beginning to work, Selina.'

She flushed. 'What? What do you mean?'

'You know what I mean. That's the first time I've ever seen you react encouragingly to a pick-up attempt. Usually you hand them off with a boat-hook, but just now you gave him the green light from the start.'

'I did nothing of the kind!' Her cheeks were burning. He was walking so fast she almost had to run to keep up with him.

He halted and looked down at her, his grey eyes dangerous. 'You know damned well you did! He fancied you, and you were flattered. It must be the first time ever. Well, get this, and get it good ... I'm not standing around watching while you test out your new-found interest in the other sex on that halfwit!'

Selina was flaming with fury by the time he finished, her eyes sparking angrily at him. 'You're out of your mind! All I did was try to be polite to a friendly stranger, and you have me in bed with him!'

'If I thought there was any real likelihood of that I'd break your neck, Selina,' he said very softly and menacingly.

Their eyes met in a long, silent war. Her breath began to come fiercely. Her veins were throbbing with a new delirium. Then he turned away and strode on, leaving her to follow him.

They got back to the villa flushed and out of breath. Ashley walked through to his own room and slammed the door. Selina marched into hers and did likewise. Joanna, setting the table in the dining-room, chuckled to herself as she moved about. All this afternoon locked in their bedroom, and now they came home like two enemies! Selina heard her voice singing incoherently in the kitchen as she was changing her dress.

With cool deliberation she selected a dress she had rarely worn before, a slender apricot sheath which fitted her body like a glove, the neckline moulded to her breasts, suspended from two fragile strips of silk, the waist curving in and then out again to cling softly to her slim hips and down over her thighs to end at the knee, in a shimmering frou-frou of layered tulle alternately apricot and pale cream.

She made up with as much care, smoothing her foundation over her skin with careful fingers. Her lipstick was a slightly darker shade of apricot; her eyeshadow a muted sage green which emphasised the colour of her wide eyes.

When she came out on to the terrace, swaying on cream stiletto shoes, Ashley was sipping a drink by the wall. He turned casually and his eyes widened.

Selina joined him, her lashes lowered while she watched him through them discreetly.

'Can I have a drink?'

He poured her one and put it into her hand. The cool touch of his fingers made her pulses flame.

She sipped her drink, the ice clinking against the glass. He stared out across the darkening garden. A moon as big as a dinner plate was swimming above the sea, its whiteness reflected on the misty waters. The air was warm and slumbrous. She felt the atmosphere affecting her nerves.

'I wonder what Joanna has for dinner tonight?' she asked lightly. 'I'm starving.'

'Good,' said Ashley, his tone abstracted.

He wasn't even aware of her presence, she thought, looking at his hard profile with angry hostility. She had gone to so much trouble dressing up for him and now he wouldn't even look at her! She felt like hitting him to get his attention.

Joanna came out on the terrace, her expression amused and sly. 'Dinner's ready on the table,' she told them in her lilting island voice. 'Cold table tonight.'

'That's fine,' Ashley said calmly. 'You can get home to Amos now, Joanna. Thanks.'

She grinned at him, her dark eyes filled with secret laughter. 'Okay, sir!'

They went through to the cool dining-room and took their seats at the table. Silver-branched candlesticks flickered between them, the twisty red candles slightly smoking. A bottle of white wine was chilling in a bucket of ice, swathed in a white damask napkin. There were cold meats of various kinds arranged in slices on a flat platter. Cheese, salad and fruit made up the rest of the meal.

Ashley lifted the wine out and poured some into his own glass, sipped it thoughtfully, then poured Selina a full glass. She watched him pour his own and settle the bottle back among the ice with a crunching sound.

He turned back to her, lifted his glass and said softly, 'To the future.'

She blushed and drank, a faint smile in her eyes. Apparently his anger with her over the meeting in the town had completely gone.

They ate in silence for a while until Ashley said, 'There's something missing.' and got up to leave the room. A few moments later the sound of soft music filtered through from the next room, and he reappeared with a mocking smile, resuming his seat.

A curious trembling began in the pit of Selina's stomach. Was all this candlelight, wine and soft music leading up to seduction? He had said he would give her time, had promised to be patient, but he had not been patient or kind this afternoon when she was merely polite to a friendly young stranger. His reaction had been jealous, possessive and violent.

It was the dark streak of sexual violence in him which always frightened her, that implicit sexual promise in his lean body and powerful hands made her shiver.

It was true that one part of her mind wanted to have him touch her. She found him deeply attractive, just as she always had, and the three years that had elapsed between their last meeting and the present had brought about some alteration in her reactions towards him.

When he was passive, allowing her to kiss him without trying to respond, some blockage in her mind seemed to clear and she became possessed of a fevered desire for him. But as soon as he came to life and took the initiative, the old fear came rushing back.

It was the threat of sexual violence that terrified her every time.

He had finished his meal and sat back, eyeing her

enigmatically. She flushed, wondering absurdly if he could read her mind. But all he said was, 'I'll make the coffee.'

'Let me,' she said, jumping up too quickly. Her plate crashed to the floor, shattering, spilling food everywhere. Her cheeks burned with hot embarrassment. 'I'm sorry ...' she muttered, diving down to pick up the pieces.

'Leave it,' Ashley said angrily, pulling her to her feet. 'And stop saying you're sorry. I'm sick of the word!'

She looked at him anxiously. 'I can clear it before I make the coffee ...'

'Joanna can do it tomorrow. That's what she's paid for.'

'I can't leave it there all night,' she protested in dismay.

'Why not? We'll make the coffee together,' he said, propelling her towards the kitchen.

She moved about, making the coffee, while he assembled the cups. When they brushed against each other her nerves fluttered and his glance grew more and more sardonic, until at last he caught her by the wrist and said tightly, 'Stop it, Selina!'

'What?' She looked at him in confusion.

'Stop working yourself into a lather every time I come near you,' he said scornfully. 'I thought we'd got past that by now. You've been as jumpy as hell all evening—that's why you smashed that plate. You're as panic-stricken as ever. Why?'

She tugged at her wrist, held in that implacable grip. 'I don't know, but you aren't making it any better by manhandling me ...'

'Manhandling you?' He laughed harshly. 'You don't know what you're saying! If I did what I want to do right now you'd have something to be frightened about.' His eyes were leaping with fire as he looked down at her.

She froze, her lips parted in stunned apprehension. 'No, Ashley,' she whispered, shivering.

'For God's sake,' he muttered, pulling her wrist so that she fell towards him. 'You're driving me out of my mind ...'

She put out a hand to push him away, but his free arm came round her so tightly that she was crushed against him, her body bent back to lift her face towards his.

He held her like that, staring into her shifting, nervous, flickering eyes.

'You're so beautiful, Selina,' he said softly. 'Is all the fire in your hair? Or is it frozen inside you waiting to be called into life?'

She stared up at him, her eyes helplessly fixed on his hard, cruel, irresistible mouth.

It moved lower and she moaned, her lids closing to shut the sight.

Then his lips touched her, and her body shook at that first touch, as if he had set a match to her and sent her flaming into orbit. Without even knowing it she gave a tiny sigh of immense pleasure against his mouth, and her body yielded to the hard pressure of his, her hand creeping round his neck to touch his hair. His kiss flared demandingly, parting her lips. The desperate, undiminishing hunger of his kiss fed on her unwilling response, draining all her energy, all her resistance, until she was weakly lying against him, her senses leaping with insistent desire.

The bubbling of the percolator passed unnoticed. His hands slid over the apricot chiffon, caressing her, sliding the thin straps down so that he could bend his head to kiss her bare shoulders. She swayed, moaning half in protest, half in ecstatic pleasure.

He moved one hand round to her back and she heard her zip slide down. Then her dress fell away and she stood in her filmy white slip, confused and trembling, but still unresisting. Ashley lowered his head again to spread his plunder along the golden smoothness of her shoulders to her half-exposed breasts. She could feel the urgency growing inside him. Against her body his heart was thudding as if he were dying.

'Oh, God, I want you,' he muttered hoarsely, his face buried between her breasts. His hand slid up to stroke her, moving in between her flesh and the thin material covering her. She felt his fingers touch her nipple. It hardened beneath his touch and she moaned again, trembling more than ever.

Then suddenly there was the click of straw sandals on the floor in the dining-room and they sprang apart, their faces flushed and dazed.

Selina picked up her dress and fled through the door into the terrace. She ran along the terrace into her own bedroom and sank down on the bed.

She was torn between hysterical laughter and wild tears. Joanna had come just at the wrong moment. Or the right moment?

Whichever it was, she had come just in time to halt the inevitable progress of their lovemaking. Selina knew with fatal certainty that in another five minutes she would have been past recovery.

She flung herself down on her pillow. 'Oh, God,' she moaned into it huskily. 'I don't even want him to stop ... I wish Joanna didn't have such a strong sense of duty!'

CHAPTER FIVE

AFTER a while she got up from the bed and hung up her dress. Would Ashley come in search of her? She knew from her own aroused hunger that he must want to go on from where they had left-off. She stared at herself in the mirror, her wide, slanting green eyes feverishly bright against the pallor of her skin. Her lower lip trembled. She wanted him to come ... and she was terrified he would. She wasn't ready yet. It was too soon.

If he came ... would she resist him? Or would that sweet, pulsating hunger flood over her, drowning her fear and bringing about total surrender?

Already she could feel the familiar tightening of her muscles, the involuntary stiffening of her limbs at the thought of him making love to her.

How was it possible to love and hate at the same time? Part of her seemed to melt in golden pleasure at the thought of Ashley's hands on her. The other rose in angry rejection, hating him.

She opened a drawer and got out a nightdress, flinging it on the bed in a filmy, drifting heap. Then she walked through to the shower, stripped and stood, her arms lifted to her red-gold hair, slowly revolving under the caressing needles of warm water. She felt sticky and unclean. She felt that the water washed away all the dark memories, the misery and the fear. The water soaked her hair, turning it dark. Her slender body slowly relaxed in the warmth, her eyes half closed in sensual enjoyment.

When the door to the cubicle opened her eyes flew open and she stiffened, her hands instinctively taking up a protective posture, angrily saying, 'Ashley, get out!'

He was ready for bed too, wearing a short black robe tied at the waist beneath which she saw black silk pyjamas.

But although her eyes quickly flicked over him, registering that fact, it was his face which made the real impact. The grey eyes were burning on her slender nakedness. He was pale and grimly intent, his jaw tight, his mouth a thin line.

'My God, you're beautiful,' he said thickly.

'Please . . .' she whispered, shaking. 'Go away!'

Slowly he undid the belt of his robe and shrugged out of the garment, shedding his pyjamas at the same time. As he moved towards her she gave a short scream of unmistakable terror, cringing away against the tiled wall.

He took a deep breath, his face darkening with rage. 'For heaven's sake, Selina, don't be a little fool!' His hand jerked her forward into the spray of the water.

'I'm not going to force you,' he said at her ear. 'We're going to take a shower together. What's wrong with that? We swam together today, didn't we? You weren't scared then.'

She lifted her head, her eyes closing as the water ran down her face, flattening her hair to her head. Her foot slipped on the wet tiles and she grabbed at him to support herself, feeling an electric shock as her hands touched the smooth wetness of his shoulders.

The water ran down his dark head, flattening his hair so that he looked like a seal, his eyes mocking her gently. His hands slid slowly down her body, arousing pulses everywhere they touched.

'It's so long since I saw you like this,' he muttered, glancing down at her whiteness against him. 'You're not frightened now, are you? I'm not threatening you with anything but a kiss or two.'

She lifted her face, closing her eyes against the intrusion of the water.

She heard him laughing at her. A drop of water splashed to her closed eyelids, and Ashley moved closer, his tongue tracing its progress from the corner of her eye to her mouth. She moaned, her arms sliding round his neck, as his lips closed possessively on hers. The water ran down their faces. She felt it on her lashes, her cheeks, her ears. There was nothing between their bodies but the cool trickle of the water. His hands were hard against her back, pressing her closer to him.

His mouth moved across her face. Against her ear he murmured, 'You know perfectly well I want you like hell, but you can stop shivering every time I come near you. I shan't try to force you. Whenever you're ready you only have to say the word. I want you to want me too.'

'Ashley,' she whispered, feeling guilty because she could see what she was doing to him.

He lifted her into his arms, her wet head against his

shoulder. 'I'm not complaining,' he said, grinning down at her. 'I'm getting somewhere this time!'

Reaching up with one hand, he turned off the shower, then carried her into the bedroom, stood her on the floor and enveloped her in a huge white bath towel. She watched him, laughing. 'You're dripping all over the carpet!'

'Too bad,' he said cheerfully. 'I'll dry you.'

'I can dry myself,' she protested.

He halted, a hand on her towel. His eyes danced mockingly. 'You won't enjoy it as much as I will,' he told her.

She blushed and he laughed again. 'We're married. Why shouldn't I see you naked?'

'Joanna might come in ...'

He made a face. 'That woman is a pest!'

Her lashes lowered and she dimpled.

He pinched her cheek. 'Never mind Joanna. Give me that towel.'

Selina permitted him to unwind it and stood, pleasurably, while he dried her thoroughly. While he dried himself she slid into her nightdress, but occasionally her eyes wandered helplessly to take a little glance at the hard, masculine body so close to her. The dark hair, the muscled toughness, sent shivers down her back.

Ashley got back into his pyjamas and robe and sat on the edge of her bed, his hand beckoning her. Reluctantly she went to him and was pulled down on his knee.

'You'll get used to me in time,' he said gently, stroking her cheek with one finger. 'I want to be so much a part of your life that I'm almost invisible.'

He would never be that, she thought secretly, remembering the wanton longings which had crept over her as she looked at his body.

'Now you can get to bed and sleep deeply,' he said. 'You needn't be afraid of anything, certainly not of me. I won't hurt you, Selina ... I'll never hurt you.'

She put out a tongue tip to touch her dry lips. His eyes narrowed on the little movement.

'I wish you wouldn't do that,' he said roughly.

She blinked, taken aback. 'What?'

He leant forward and delicately touched her mouth with the tip of his own tongue. 'That ...' he whispered.

Deep in the pit of her stomach a strange aching began. She wanted him to do it again. Her eyes slid up to his face, their expression revealing.

Ashley made a deep, protesting sound. 'Don't look at me like that or all my good intentions will fly out of the window!' He stood up, letting her slide on to the bed. 'Goodnight, Selina,' he said firmly, walking to the door.

She turned out the light and climbed into bed. Outside in the garden there were strange, unfamiliar noises. She lay listening to them, unable to sleep. Frogs were croaking somewhere; a bird hooted like a car klaxon. The sea whispered and whispered eternally under the huge tropical silver moon.

In the morning Selina was already at the breakfast table when Ashley came out on to the terrace to join her. His eyes quickly read her cool expression.

'Good morning,' she said politely.

His smile was mocking. 'Did you sleep well?'

Despite her resolution to be calm and controlled in his presence, she began to blush. 'Yes, thank you,' she said crossly. 'Did you?'

He buttered a roll. 'No,' he said casually. 'I had very pleasant dreams, though.'

She bit her lip. He was going to make it hard for her, she saw. She had betrayed herself last night. Despite his protest that he would be patient, she felt he was rushing her, and the giddy uncertainty of her own feelings needed time. She loved him, she wanted him, but if she did let him make love to her she was afraid the result would be the same as before, and she could not bear that.

'Can we go to town again today?' she asked. 'I'd like to see more of it.'

He lowered the roll as he was about to bite into it. The grey eyes narrowed. 'Why do you want to go into town?'

'Why not?' she shrugged, pouring herself a cup of coffee.

'I don't want your young admirer following us around, that's why not,' he said tersely.

'Oh, don't be absurd!'

'Is it absurd? You liked him. Do you think I didn't notice?'

'You made a fuss about nothing,' she protested. 'I was polite, nothing more.'

'You didn't see the smile you gave him,' he retorted.

She looked at him through her lashes. 'Jealousy is poisonous.'

Ashley's face tightened. 'I'm aware of that,' he said shortly.

She was suddenly sorry she had provoked the argument. She had done it to distract him from his teasing, but now she wished she hadn't.

She looked down at the table, her finger tracing a circle on the cloth. 'After all, I haven't asked you any questions about the women in your life. Don't tell me you've spent the last three years reading books and playing tennis!'

He was silent. She looked up quickly and found him staring at her with an odd expression.

'I gathered,' he said carefully, 'that you didn't much care how I'd spent the last three years. Or with whom.'

A pang of savage jealousy shot through her. She looked away again. 'I'm curious, naturally,' she said lightly.

'Curious?' The word was edged.

'It's only human.'

'Not jealous, though?' he asked sardonically.

Selina felt hot colour creeping into her cheeks. 'Why should I be?' she asked, but her voice came out huskily.

'You tell me,' he said.

She shrugged uncertainly. 'Jealousy implies possession. I didn't own you.'

'Didn't you?' The question was flung at her savagely. 'Do you think I found it easy to forget you?'

'There was Clare,' she pointed out.

He laughed bitterly. 'She was just a diversion meant to make you jealous. We parted after a few months.'

'Poor Clare,' she said sadly, remembering her tragic death.

'Don't waste your pity on her. She wasn't emotionally involved. I wasn't the first man in her life, or the last.'

'You were booked in on the same flight,' she pointed out.

'Sheer coincidence,' he shrugged. 'I cancelled my flight because I . . .' His words broke off and she looked at him quickly.

'Because you what?'

He grimaced. 'If you must have the truth, my private detective had told me Roger was in deep water again. He'd been keeping an eye on both of you and he knew about Roger's debts.'

Her mind worked swiftly and she stared at him in grim accusation. 'You came back deliberately!'

He nodded. 'I wanted to be around when you needed me.'

'You always meant to buy me back,' she said slowly, her voice shaking. 'You waited for the right opportunity. You knew Roger was bound to get into big trouble one day.'

His face was blank. 'Yes,' he said. 'You might as well know the truth. That is just what I hoped for—that you would need a lot of money really desperately. I told you once—I never give up what I own. You're mine. I knew the only way I could get you back was through Roger, so I played a waiting game.'

Selina looked at him with hatred. 'What a cold-blooded, despicable thing to do!'

His face was unreadable. 'Knowing this doesn't change anything,' he said. 'I came through when you needed me. If I hadn't been there, what would have happened to Roger? Or would you have sold yourself to some other wealthy businessman?'

The tone flicked her like a whip. She was white with rage. 'I loathe you,' she said shakily.

'I thought you were intelligent enough to take the truth,' he said. 'A pity you aren't, isn't it?'

There was a slap of sandals behind them and Joanna appeared. 'Telephone,' she said cheerfully. 'For you, Mr Dent.'

'Tell them I'm out for the day,' Ashley said tautly.

'They say it's urgent,' she told him.

'Is it long-distance?' he asked irritably.

She shook her head. 'Right here in town. A Mr Campbell.'

Ashley stood up. 'Very well, I'll take it.' He moved across the terrace with long strides and Selina turned back to her breakfast, her appetite gone.

When Ashley returned he was grim-faced. He looked at her coolly. 'I've got to go into town on business. You'll have to stay here until I get back. I shouldn't be too long.'

'Can't I come with you?' she asked resentfully. 'What am I supposed to do here all by myself?'

'Swim,' he commanded tersely. 'Sunbathe. For God's sake, Selina, there's plenty for you to do around the villa for a few hours.'

'But I want to go into town anyway,' she pointed out.

His jaw set angrily. 'Too bad—you're staying here. I don't want you wandering around a strange town on your own.'

She stood up, her eyes spitting fire at him. 'The fact that we're married doesn't give you the right to order me around!'

'Yes, it does,' he said flatly. He took hold of her elbow and hustled her back into the villa, into her bedroom. She dragged her feet, struggling, protesting in a muted way because she did not want Joanna to hear them.

'Where's that parcel I gave you?' he demanded.

She had forgotten it. It was in the bottom of the wardrobe, still wrapped, and Ashley's brows jerked together as she produced it.

'I see my presents really excite you,' he snapped. 'Couldn't you even have opened it?'

She was sorry she had not done so and to propitiate him unwrapped it there and then, exclaiming with pleasure at the bikini she found inside. Briefer than any she had ever worn, it was a smooth cream coloured cotton printed with tiny orange flowers.

'Thank you, Ashley,' she said, turning to smile at him, sorry that they had had another of their arguments.

'Put it on,' he said, his tone demanding.

She flushed, eyeing him. Did he mean to stand there and watch? His mouth quirked sardonically and he walked across to the window, turning his back.

'Is this better?'

Rapidly Selina changed into the bikini, feeling nervous as she told him he could turn round again.

His eyes drifted over her appreciatively. 'Now come and thank me properly,' he drawled, extending a hand.

Obediently she crossed the room, deeply conscious of the grey eyes watching her. Ashley pulled her against his body and bent his head. The kiss was coaxing, rather than violent, and she found no hardship in returning it, even when one of his hands moved softly along her midriff and cupped a breast. 'You're ravishing,' he whispered against her mouth. 'Beautiful, beautiful Selina ... can you blame me for wanting to keep you captive here, just for my eyes?'

'Do you have to go into town?' she asked idly, her fingers twirling one of the buttons on his shirt.

'Unfortunately, I do,' he said with regret. 'This chap Campbell is involved in a hotel deal I'm negotiating, and I can't afford to offend him. He heard I was staying at the villa from a mutual friend in the States, and as he's on the island for a week he thought he would give me a ring.' He grinned. 'He isn't aware I'm on my honeymoon, of course. I've managed to keep our marriage discreetly out of print.'

She looked at him, frowning. Was he ashamed of the marriage? Why didn't he want the papers to know about it?

'Are you going to keep me a dark secret from all your friends?' she asked pointedly.

He looked at her in surprise. 'You wouldn't want to meet Campbell. He's rather a dull chap, although very friendly. The one passion of his life is his daughter, Renata.'

'That's an unusual name,' she commented.

He grinned. 'Her mother was German. I believe the name is a German one.'

'And is Renata Campbell a beautiful Teutonic blonde?' she asked, her voice edged.

He looked down at her, the grey eyes narrowing. 'Do I detect a note of asperity in your voice?'

Selina flushed. 'Just curiosity.'

'Of course,' he said mockingly, 'I'd forgotten. You're never jealous.'

She looked away. 'Will you be back for lunch?'

'I'm not certain,' he said. 'I'll try to get away, but I may have to stay until after lunch. Campbell will think it odd if I refuse.' His eyes mocked her again. 'He probably thinks I'm here with a lady friend.'

'I'm sure he has good reason for his suspicions,' she retorted tartly.

Ashley laughed, his smile full of sudden charm. 'Careful, my darling, you're beginning to sound like a jealous woman, and you wouldn't want that, would you?'

He moved to the door before she could reply. Pausing to survey her again, he grimaced. 'You don't know how much I hate to leave you. You're totally delectable in that. I'll be back as soon as I can get away.'

Then he had gone, and Selina found a large bath towel, the sun tan lotion and a paperback, and wandered out into the villa garden. There was a pretty floral-upholstered beach swing on the lawn. Curling up on the cushions, she read her book, enjoying the peace and tranquillity of the morning.

Stretching lazily, she glanced at her watch and found it was nearly lunch time. Joanna came out on the terrace and grinned at her.

'You look nice and lazy,' she called in her soft voice. 'When do you want lunch, Mrs Dent? I get it whenever you like. Mr Dent not coming back?'

'If he isn't here we're to start without him,' she said. 'I'll just have salad and fruit, thank you, Joanna.'

Over the meal she talked to Joanna about her family and her life on the island. Feeling like a short nap, she then walked down to the beach and stretched out on the sand, her new beach hat shading her from the worst of the midday sun.

Then footsteps crunched along the sand near her she turned lazily, a welcoming smile breaking out on her mouth, expecting to see Ashley. It was not him, however. Her smile wavered as she recognised the young man they had met the day before.

'Oh, hello,' she said uncertainly.

His friendly beam widened. 'Hi! Remember me? We met in the town. I'm Phil Webster.'

'I remember,' she said politely. 'You know my brother.'

He stood looking down at her, warm admiration in his eyes. 'I wish I'd known Roger had such a pretty sister,' he said frankly. 'I would have asked for an invitation to meet you.'

She laughed, amused by his directness. 'I am married, you know,' she pointed out. 'In fact, we're on our honeymoon.'

His eyes widened. 'Good lord? Really? What a close shave!'

'A close shave?' She was puzzled, but still amused. 'How do you mean?'

'If I'd met you before you met your husband it might be us on our honeymoon,' he said cheerfully.

Selina laughed, her eyes dancing. 'You take a lot for granted, Mr Webster.'

He caught on at once. 'You don't think you would have fancied me that much?' He sighed. 'I suppose I'm not any sort of competition for your husband. Bit awesome, isn't he?'

'Talking of my husband,' she said gently, 'he might be back any minute and if he found you here he might be angry. This is a private beach, you know.'

Phil Webster lowered himself beside her, unabashed. 'He won't be back for quite a while,' he said confidently.

'How can you be so sure?'

'I saw him starting to eat an enormous lunch at the Lorelei Hotel,' he said brightly. 'He was with a bald-headed old chap and an absolutely stunning peach of a girl ...' His eyes swivelled to catch Selina's expression. 'Not as lovely as you, mind you,' he said hastily. 'But beauty queen material, all the same.'

Her stomach turned over jealously. 'It is a business

lunch,' she said, and wondered why she felt impelled to make excuses for Ashley. If he wanted to have lunch with a peach of a girl that was his problem, not hers. She didn't care if he had lunch with a dozen assorted beauty queens. But why hadn't he told her that Renata Campbell was with her father on the island? He must have known. Was that why he had dashed off at a moment's notice?

Phil Webster was gazing, entranced, at her bikini. 'Are you going to swim?' he asked. 'Would you mind if I join you?'

She glanced at his T-shirt and pale blue jeans. 'Have you got swimming trunks with you?'

He nodded. 'Under this.'

She shrugged. 'I suppose it doesn't matter.' Why should Ashley expect her to wait here alone while he lunched with stunning girls? What was sauce for the gander was certainly sauce for the goose!

Suddenly for some reason the prospect of arousing his jealousy was not an unpleasant one. It satisfied some urge in her to punish him for having left her to lunch with another woman, especially a stunning peach of a blonde. Clare Leslie had been a blonde. Selina had hated her on sight, envying her the uncomplicated sexuality which could respond to Ashley without fear or shame.

She stood up and walked down the beach, the sand burning under her feet. Wading into the blue, blue water she heard Phil running down behind her, muttering as the soles of his feet came in contact with hot sand.

They swam out together lazily and then turned and drifted on their backs, their arms spread wide to balance themselves. The coolness of the water was refreshing.

'Have you ever noticed how white people's legs look in the sea?' Phil asked her, gazing at her slender body with open pleasure. 'Is it an optical illusion, do you think? Or is it the salt in the water?'

She dived and swam towards the beach, saying over her shoulder, 'I've no idea ... race you!'

He followed and drew level with her, grinning at her as he shot ahead.

He was waiting as she ran up out of the waves, his eyes bright, his dripping hair falling over his temples.

'Do I get a prize?' he asked impudently. 'Races should always have prizes.'

She scooped up a piece of odd-coloured seaweed and threw it at him. 'Yes, here it is.'

It wrapped itself around his face, and while he was unpeeling it, laughing, Selina ran past him up the beach, snatched up her towel and bolted for the wicket gate.

Phil caught her as she reached it and his arm slid round her waist. 'That was a filthy trick,' he said lightly. 'You owe me a kiss for that.'

She was suddenly angry, her eyes turning to green ice diamonds as she looked up at him.

But before she could speak, another voice bit out savagely, 'What the hell is going on here?'

Phil released her, going pale. 'Sorry ...' he stammered, eyeing Ashley nervously. 'Just ... just fun ...' Then he turned and vanished like a rabbit.

Coward, she thought, watching his disappearing figure with scorn. He had left her to face the music. She turned and looked at Ashley, her heart turning over at the look on his face.

She had not seen him so angry for days. The old violence was back in his eyes. He was poised like a rattlesnake for the kill, his whole body tense and savage.

Selina looked at him wearily, pushing a trembling hand through her wet red-gold hair. 'I found him on our beach,' she said nervously. 'He hasn't been here long.'

'Long enough,' he bit out. 'What would have happened if I hadn't arrived so inopportunely? You're alone with him for an hour ... it can't have been much longer, because I saw him in town an hour and a half ago and it would have taken him some time to get out here ... but that's all it takes, apparently, for him to get around to kissing you without even a token resistance on your part!'

'He hadn't kissed me,' she denied quickly.

'He was going to!'

'I wouldn't have let him,' she said.

'That wasn't how it looked to me.' Ashley's voice deepened into black fury. 'To me it looked as if you were standing there inviting it.'

'That's not true!' Her face grew flushed.

Ashley strode over to her and caught her by the wrist, his fingers cruel. 'I must be insane,' he said, as if to himself, staring into her face. 'While I play Patience on a monument and wait for you to turn to me, some little swine comes along and you drop into his eager hand like a ripe peach ...'

'Ashley, that's unfair!'

Her words were ignored. He scooped her up into his arms and walked rapidly up the garden to the house with her. Joanna came out on the terrace and beamed at them, then looked puzzled as Ashley speechlessly passed her and carried Selina through the open french windows to her own bedroom.

His foot slammed the door hard behind him. He strode to the bed and dumped her unceremoniously on it, then moved back to the door and locked it.

'Ashley ...' His name strangled in her throat. She stared at him in shock and dismay as he began to take off his clothes, his dark face angrily set.

Scrambling off the bed, she turned and bolted for the window, intending to climb out on to the terrace, but he was behind her before she reached it. His hands were merciless as he pulled her back against him. She jumped in shock, feeling the hard naked flesh touch hers, but he was turning her round to face him, his fingers locking themselves into her damp hair.

'Don't do this, please,' she begged weakly. 'I'm wet ... what will Joanna think ...' Then, on a wild cry of protest, 'No, Ashley!'

His mouth took relentless possession of hers, parting her lips. His hands were everywhere, touching her desirously, his fingertips caressing, and a sudden shiver of response ran through her. When his hands unhooked her bikini top, and then the briefs, she only moaned faintly, her protest purely habit. From somewhere deep inside her a tidal wave of sexual yearning rose and crashed down, drowning her fear.

As if he sensed the change, his touch softened. When he lifted her into his arms, his hands beneath her knees and back, she made no attempt to escape, her face turned upward for his searching kiss, her hands locked round his neck.

He laid her on the bed and slid down beside her, his

mouth finding her breast. The warm, lazy seductive movement went on and on until she was totally mindless, her hand going to the back of his dark head to hold him there.

He moved up to kiss her mouth again, and the warm pressure of their bodies grew. She felt herself overtaken by a deep, persistent ache which could only be satisfied by surrender. Blind with a passion she had never known before, her mouth opened against his, her hands touching him ardently.

'Tell me you want me,' he whispered against her mouth. 'I want to hear you say it ...'

'I want you,' she admitted weakly. She had forgotten how this all began. The rage, the savagery, were forgotten. All she knew was that for the first time in her life she was lost to everything but the burning demands of her own body, and only Ashley could ever satisfy them.

His long sigh seemed to drain him. For a moment he lay there, his face against her throat, breathing hard. She could hear his heart beating so fast she was almost frightened. Suddenly he pulled away, leaning over her on his elbow.

'I said I wouldn't force you,' he said huskily. 'This is your last chance. I'm not beyond reason at the moment, but if you aren't certain say so and I'll get out of this room before I lose control again.'

She looked at him, her tongue tip touching her lower lip, trying to discover her own reactions. For a moment she had forgotten everything but him. Why had he stopped, putting doubt back into her troubled mind?

'For God's sake, Selina,' he burst out harshly, staring

at her pink tongue as it caressed her lip. 'Make up your damned mind, or I'll go mad!'

She half closed her eyes to shut out the disturbing darkness of his face. 'How can I think when you look at me like that?'

His breath caught audibly in the back of his throat. 'Selina,' he groaned. 'Oh, God . . .' His mouth lowered to hers again, so fiercely that she gasped. The burning kiss set a torch to her own feelings, making her quiver in helpless response. Against her mouth he whispered, 'Don't refuse me this time . . . my darling, let me love you . . .'

Before she had time to consider anything he began to kiss her shoulders, covering her with light butterfly kisses that tantalised and excited her. When his mouth moved lower, whispering her name between kisses, she was thrown into a vortex of unexpected, unknown sensuality, her head thrashing from side to side, her mouth open in a moan of pleasure.

The savagery of sexual possession which she had always feared so deeply seemed a world away from this expert, deliberate seduction. The brushing, teasing softness of his mouth drove her insane. 'Darling, darling,' she whispered crazily, utterly lost to everything but her love for him.

Suddenly her body stiffened, all that warm, responsive relaxation torn by pain. Icy waves of panic broke over her. Ashley's mouth was on hers, but the softly yielding body which had provoked his invasion was suddenly fighting tooth and nail for freedom. She sobbed as she struggled, her nails raking his shoulders, her body tossing beneath his in bitter rejection. She lost all consciousness of him as the man she loved; he was merely an aggressor, a cruel, faceless enemy whose assault drove her into terror.

She moaned out pleas for him to stop, her voice choked with fear and hatred, but now he was as blind in the grip of primitive emotion as herself. His hands held her savagely beneath him, pinioning her flailing hands. She could hear the thudding of his heart against her, the gasping agony of his breathing, and above them both the hoarse voice whispering her name again and again.

Then she was free, shivering, sobbing, filled with incredulous rage. She rolled away from him, hating him as she listened to his breathing slowing from that fierce, ragged intake of air to a slower rhythm.

After a moment he touched her shoulder gently, but she shrugged his hand away. 'Don't touch me!'

'Selina ...' he pleaded gently.

'I hate you,' she whispered. 'Don't ever come near me again or I'll kill you!'

He was still for a while, then he spoke quietly. 'I'm sorry it happened, too, Selina. I didn't mean it to happen like this. I warned you not to play with my feelings. Yesterday afternoon and then again tonight you deliberately invited me to make love to you ...'

'No!' she cried furiously.

'God, what do you think I'm made of? Stone?'

'You hurt me,' she accused in a low, bitter tone.

He groaned. 'I know, my darling. There was no way I could avoid it. Next time ...'

'There'll never be a next time. I'll never let you touch me again,' she said fiercely.

He spun her round contemptuously. 'We made a bargain, remember? I would have gone on being patient for as long as it took, but I'm not the sort of man who'll stand by and watch his wife flirting with another man, especially when she isn't even prepared to make the marriage a real one!'

'You promised you wouldn't force me to do anything I didn't want to do,' she reminded him.

'I meant it,' he said grimly. 'But that was before I realised you were trying to get some sort of sexual revenge on the whole male sex by tantalising me and then pulling back before the brink ... you thought you had me just where you wanted me, didn't you? You behaved like a naughty child watching something squirming on a pin.'

'That's a vile thing to say!'

'Is it?' His eyes were deadly. 'Ever since we got here you've been indulging in some pretty cold-blooded teasing. You enjoyed watching me go up in flames, but you had no intention of getting caught in the con-flagration.'

'That's not true!'

'Isn't it, Selina? Can you deny that you teased me to the point of madness last night, knowing perfectly well that you never intended to let me go further than a few kisses?'

She was flushed and angry now, yet inwardly con-fused. It was true that it had given her a sense of power to see that dark look of passion in his eyes, to hear him breathe hard as he kissed her. She hadn't intended to tease or provoke him, though. In fact, she had been just as excited herself, her whole body on fire under his touch.

'You're just counter-attacking, to make me forget the way you broke your word,' she accused.

'It never occurred to me until I saw the way you stood there, inviting that young puppy to kiss you,' he said bitterly. 'You'd been playing the same game with him, I imagine ... a pretty sick game, don't you think? And just now, you were responding passionately until I took you. If you'd been as frightened as you claim, you would have stopped me long before I got to that point.'

'I ... hadn't expected it to hurt so much,' she said, her eyes miserable.

'You mean you hadn't expected I would get that far,' he said bitingly. 'What was the matter, Selina? Did you actually get a little carried away yourself for once? Did your iron control slip just long enough for me to be beyond the point of no return?'

'Stop it!' she said furiously. 'I'm not like that.'

'Aren't you?' His lip lifted in a sneer. 'You're going to have to prove that to me, my dear.'

Wondering what he meant, she watched helplessly as he stood up and began to get dressed again. Shamefully she felt her body tense in sudden awareness of his powerful sexuality and hurriedly looked away from the muscled virility of his lean body.

He finished dressing and stared at her grimly, his hands deep in his pockets. 'Look in the mirror and you'll see a woman who's been made love to very passionately,' he said. 'And that's what you are, my dear. What we did wasn't disgusting or ugly; it was natural and beautiful, an act of love.'

'*We* did?' she questioned involuntarily, and regretted it was too late as she saw the tide of dark red that ran up his face, realising that her words had stung his masculine pride.

'All right,' he said tensely. 'I was solely responsible

for what happened, if that's how you prefer to see it. You just lay there and suffered my disgusting attentions. But if you now imagine that you've fulfilled your side of our bargain, let me disillusion you. Ten thousand pounds would be an exorbitant price for the pleasure of making love to you just once, enjoyable though the process was ... I intend to exact full payment from you, Selina.' The grey eyes flickered over her, from her pink mouth, full and moistly bloomed from his kisses, along the naked curve of golden shoulder, breast and thigh, making her wince at the bitter mixture of contempt and deliberate sensual desire he allowed her to see. 'You belong to me. I own you.' The tight phrases were bitten out savagely. 'I'll never let you get away from me again. From now on I'll take you when and how I choose, and you'll submit without protest.' The grey eyes lifted to her face again, coldly challenging her to argue. 'Is that understood?'

'Am I expected to enjoy it, too?' she asked bitterly.

Ashley bent and jerked her to her feet, his hands cruel. Crushing her against him, his mouth savaged her, deliberately using every ounce of force. She struggled, trying to pull her head aside, but then the kiss altered and grew slow and seductive, coaxing her bruised lips apart, and to her chagrin and self-disgust she could sense herself weakening, responding, wanting him.

When at last he lifted his head there was triumph in every line of his body. The glittering eyes mocked her. 'Yes,' he said huskily, 'you will enjoy it, too.'

Flushed and trembling, she pulled the sheet from her bed and wrapped it around herself, her head bent to avoid his gaze.

'We're going out to dinner tonight,' he said, watching her. 'I thought it best to mention our marriage to Mr Campbell and he asked to meet you. Wear something special.' He glanced into her wardrobe casually. 'That yellow thing will do.'

Selina looked at the apricot dress hanging just inside the open door. 'I wore that last night.'

'I am well aware that you did,' he said softly. 'You looked enchanting in it, as you know very well.' Turning away, he strolled to the door, unlocked and opened it.

'Will Mr Campbell's daughter be there tonight?' she asked.

He glanced back and a mocking smile curled his lips. 'Yes,' he said lightly. 'She will.'

CHAPTER SIX

THE Lorelei Hotel was a large white rambling building rather reminiscent of American Colonial style, with tall pillars supporting the terrace roof, palm-leaf shaped wicker chairs grouped around low tables, green lawns kept fresh and cool by a hidden sprinkler system, flower beds a riot of unbelievable gaudy colour and a general air of being without purpose and meaning even for the tourists grouped around the large outdoor swimming pool.

'It looks like a film set,' Selina said idly, staring around her as she stood on the terrace facing the pool. Among the people splashing in the bright blue water

she saw Phil Webster, and she knew that he saw her
from the way he very carefully looked the other way.
Ashley's brooding presence at her shoulder was clearly
too much for him.

'Your ... friend ... seems determined to pretend he
doesn't see us,' Ashley drawled derisively. 'You seem
to collect cowardly boys. He reminds me of your
brother.'

'Discretion is the better part of valour,' she said,
shrugging. 'I imagine he feels embarrassed.'

'As well he might,' said Ashley. 'If he comes near you
again I'll break his neck.'

A voice greeted them and they both turned. Selina's
eyes passed briefly over the middle-aged man who came
forward with outstretched hands to touch on his companion with a little thrust of nervous apprehension.

In that one comprehensive glance she saw enough to
increase her anxiety. Renata Campbell was a glowing,
golden girl with great blue eyes, elegant long legs and a
warm, caressing smile which at this moment was unmistakably fixed on Ashley.

'Mr Campbell, may I present my wife. Selina, this is
Mr Campbell, who has been kind enough to ask us to
dinner.' Ashley had his hand beneath her elbow as he
made the introduction, and the slight, possessive
gesture left no doubt in the minds of the other two
people present that he regarded her as his possession.
There was something in the way he stood beside her,
constantly aware of her, that reinforced the implicit
declaration of ownership. She was deeply conscious of
it herself, and saw Renata's long, narrowed glance
harden on her.

Lifting her chin, she smiled and shook hands with Mr

Campbell, turned to repeat the process with Renata. The other girl's hand was limp between her fingers and quickly withdrawn.

'We had no idea Ashley was married or we would never have got in touch with him,' said Mr Campbell, his bald head shining with the heat. He had Renata's blue eyes, slightly protuberant in his case, and a kind, warm smile which softened the otherwise aggressive cut of his features. 'Renata always accuses me of being obsessed with business, but even I draw the limit at butting in on another man's honeymoon . . . I asked you and your husband to dinner, Mrs Dent, so that I could apologise in person, and after tonight we'll vanish from your lives, I promise.'

'I hope you will do nothing of the kind,' Ashley returned with equal formality. 'When we fly home I shall be very happy to see you visiting us for dinner very soon.'

Mr Campbell laughed. 'You're a very forgiving man, Ashley. I don't think I would feel too kindly to anyone who interrupted my honeymoon, especially if my wife was as lovely as yours!' And he smiled at Selina admiringly.

'What unusual hair,' Renata said softly. 'I've never seen that particular colour before.' Her eyes were cold as she stared at Selina and the implication was clear— she meant that she suspected Selina's hair to be artificially coloured to that shade of red-gold.

Selina smiled coolly at her. 'Thank you,' she said with extreme courtesy, pretending to believe it to be a compliment.

'Shall we go in and have an aperitif?' Mr Campbell asked quickly, as if nervous of what his daughter might

say next. 'Mrs Dent, may I have the pleasure?' He
crooked his arm, smiling, and Selina moved to join him.
Renata softly slipped past her to take Ashley's arm
between her two hands, smiling up at him invitingly. It
was extraordinary, thought Selina, how that smile could
change. When it was focused on Ashley it was like a
naked electric light. The warmth vanished, however,
when she turned to look at Ashley's wife. Had Mr
Campbell's presence on the island been purely coincidence? Or had Renata been aware of Ashley's presence
here, if not of his marriage? Had she in fact deliberately pursued him here with the intention of getting
to know him better? It must have been something of a
shock to her to find out that he was married.

The cocktail bar was dimly lit and exotically decor-
ated with potted palms, conch shells, fishing nets draped
across the walls with starfish and pearly pink shells
fixed among their folds, and a general air of unreal
native colour. Mr Campbell fussed over Selina, seeing
her comfortably settled in a deep white leather chair,
while Renata slid down on to a high-backed leather
couch opposite, patting the place next to her with a
smile at Ashley, who sat down next to her, his thigh
obviously pressing her slim leg. Briefly his glance
flickered to Selina, taunting her, but she withdrew her
own gaze before it had met his and turned to smile at
Mr Campbell.

A waiter materialised, bowing, and Mr Campbell
asked her what she would like to drink.

'That dress is really something,' Mr Campbell said as
the waiter moved away. 'What colour would you call
that?'

'Apricot,' she said softly.

'It suits you,' he nodded. 'Same colour as your skin.'

She laughed. 'I shall be the colour of that wood when we get home, the sun is so hot here.'

He considered her. 'With your colouring you shouldn't be out in the sun too long, you know, although you're so brown I don't suppose it will matter much.'

Renata was murmuring so softly to Ashley that Selina could not hear a word, but the undisguised intimacy between the two of them was making her seethe angrily. He was doing this deliberately.

The drinks arrived, and she sipped hers carefully, listening to Mr Campbell's voice without really hearing what he said. Her whole being was concentrated on the two opposite them, although she never once glanced in their direction. Antennae she had not known she possessed picked up every tone of voice, every slight movement between them, and she was deeply, bitterly angry with Ashley for the way he was behaving.

They eventually ordered their meal, sipping their drinks and quietly discussing the menu, and ten minutes later a waiter arrived to invite them to take their places at the table.

As they walked through the bar into the more brightly lit dining-room Selina's eyes caught the glance of a stranger across the room and for one split second her body was wrung by a sensation of revulsion and shock.

The thin, brown face and silvered hair, the air of authority undisguised beneath a lightweight suit, were hatefully familiar to her, and her widened eyes conveyed as much to the man watching her across the tables.

Then she turned away to follow her party to their table, allowing Mr Campbell to fuss over her once more as she sat down. Her hands shook as she shook out her napkin. Her lips were dry with sudden appalling tension.

Ashley, glancing at her, frowned, his eyes narrowing. He looked around the room in a swift, searching glance, then looked back at her, his eyes searching, demanding an explanation. Selina could feel the draining of her colour. Her fingers were icy cold and shook as she gripped the edge of the table.

Swallowing, she managed to begin her meal, although she had never felt less like eating. The food tasted like sawdust and her throat closed in revulsion as she forced it down.

During the second course her attention was caught when the man at the other side of the room stood up and moved towards their table. Her nerves leapt in terrified anticipation, although she never once looked at him. He slowed as he neared them, his eyes fixed on her averted face. Ashley laid down his fork, staring at her in hard enquiry.

The tall, thin man paused beside their table, his eyes fixed on her.

For a few seconds longer Selina tried not to turn and look at him, but his insistence was unavoidable. At last she slowly moved her head and their eyes met.

Pulses were beating painfully at her throat and wrist. Her wide, terrified eyes pleaded with him.

He bowed, his face expressionless. 'Good evening, Selina,' he said calmly. Without even looking at her companions he then moved away and left the dining-room.

She looked down at her plate, her lips shaking. She knew that Ashley was staring at her, and she did not need to look at him to know the expression in his grey eyes.

Renata Campbell was alert, picking up the tension at the table. 'A friend of yours, Mrs Dent?' she asked softly.

Selina forced herself to look up. A wide, mirthless smile moved her mouth. 'Not exactly,' she said huskily. 'I . . . I met him once, years ago.'

'You obviously made a deep impression,' Renata laughed with the tinkling sound of ice.

'I'm not surprised,' Mr Campbell said, smiling bluffly. 'His face is familiar. What does he do, Mrs Dent? He isn't an actor, is he? He has that sort of face.'

'He was rather dishy, in an austere sort of way,' Renata commented. She looked sideways at Ashley, her long mouth curved in a teasing smile. 'If I were on my honeymoon I think I'd resent the way he stared at Mrs Dent. Underneath that unbending exterior I got the impression he fancied your wife, Ashley.'

Selina was trying desperately not to let her eyes meet Ashley's. She could feel his insistent gaze in every nerve of her body. But when he spoke his voice drawled calmly. 'If I got worked up about every man who looks at my wife I'd be in a permanent lather,' he said.

Renata laughed. 'That's a very civilised attitude! I'm not sure I'd like my husband to be that complacent.'

Selina was not fooled by Ashley's light dismissal of the subject. She could feel the impact of his anger although their eyes never met.

The waiter hovered to refill their glasses, and somehow the subject altered to a discussion of the local scenery. The meal progressed ceremonially. Selina managed to eat some of the food placed before her, aware that lack of appetite on her part would draw down comment. She was grateful to Renata now for holding Ashley's attention. At least while he was talking to the other girl he was not watching her in that remorseless fashion, and she had time to consider the cruelty of fate which had brought that man here tonight.

The fact that he had not only recognised her, but remembered her name, appalled her.

He must have an incredible memory. Surely she must have changed out of all recognition in the years since they last met? Yet he had known her at once. As she had him, of course, but she had much greater reason to remember him in graphic detail, and to hate him more than any man she had ever met. The cold, probing cruel eyes, the slight sneer on his pale mouth, the beautiful remorseless voice were all bitterly familiar to her. She had dreamt about him for years. For a moment, seeing him across that room, she had felt she was falling back into those hellish nightmares, and perspiration had broken out along her spine.

They finished their meal at last and Mr Campbell glanced at his watch. 'Now I realise you two have already spent a great deal of time on us, but I'd be grateful if you have a last drink with us before you leave.'

Ashley sounded tense as he replied. 'That's very kind of you, but . . .'

Renata broke in swiftly, 'Oh, please, you can't go yet! The night's still young and they have a marvellous band in the Grotto Room. There's absolutely no one to dance with me and I was hoping you would want to dance for a little while.'

Selina risked glancing at them, and saw Ashley staring down into the other girl's wide, appealing blue eyes. A faint smile curved his hard mouth. 'How can I resist such an invitation?'

Absurdly, Selina was torn between jealousy and a feeling of relief. She was not looking forward to being alone with Ashley. His questions would be unavoidable and she did not want to talk about the stranger who was so familiar to her.

The Grotto Room was octagonal in shape, lined with the same white leather couches as the bar, but with the centre of the room cleared for dancing and a raised dais at one end on which a small group of musicians were playing rhythmically. Half a dozen couples were dancing, but most of the couches were occupied with people drinking.

They found a table and sat down. Mr Campbell clicked his finger and thumb towards the circulating waiter and he hurried over. Renata stood up again, saying, 'Order for us, Daddy,' and her hand pulled at Ashley. 'Let's dance,' she said frankly, her eyes full of warm invitation.

Selina resented the way she slid into Ashley's arms and moved away with him, her slim body curved against him, the golden head close to his cheek. Over her shoulder Ashley stared back at Selina. She looked away, her lashes resting on her brown skin.

'You mustn't mind Renata,' said Mr Campbell, a little uncomfortably. 'She's spoilt, I guess, but she doesn't mean any harm. She just naturally flirts with any good-looking man she meets.' His eyes were apologetic. 'It doesn't mean a thing!'

'Of course not,' Selina said quietly, forcing a polite smile.

Their drinks arrived and she sipped at hers, watching

the band rather than do what she wanted to do, which was watch Ashley. She would not give him that satisfaction. If he wanted to punish her by flirting with Renata she would make sure he never caught a look of jealousy in her eyes.

Mr Campbell was talking about the hotel business, laughing as he described his latest venture, and Selina listened courteously, her mind only partially on what he said.

The music ended and Ashley and Renata returned to the table to claim their drinks. Renata was flushed and smiling, obviously well pleased with her dance. 'You dance better than any man I ever met,' she told Ashley, her hand resting on his thigh.

Selina could not help staring at that slim brown hand. Her glance lifted to Ashley's face and met the narrowed gaze of the grey eyes. He made no effort to move away, or to dislodge Renata's hand from his leg.

The music struck up again and Renata put down her glass, standing up with glowing eyes. 'Shall we?'

'Renata!' Mr Campbell looked shocked. 'Ashley's wife may want to dance this one.'

Renata's lower lip pouted. Her eyes looked at Selina with acute dislike. But at that instant a newcomer appeared beside the table, his face guarded as he looked down at Selina.

'May I have this dance?'

Her whole body tensed as if at a blow. She looked at him helplessly, longing to refuse yet not daring to do so. Slowly she stood up and walked with him to the dance floor.

As his arm slid round her waist she shivered, caught in a nightmare terror.

He looked down at her, his other hand taking hers. 'Don't look at me like that,' he said in that beautiful, cold voice. 'I know how you must view me, but I've wanted to see you again for years to tell you how sorry I was to have to treat you the way I did.'

She was somehow moving with him, her body automatically following his smooth movements, Tensely, her voice hoarse, she said, 'Are you actually apologising to me, Sir Daniel?'

'Yes,' he said gently. 'And trying to explain. It was the obvious ... indeed, the only line of defence ... and I think you must have realised that my client himself put it forward most strongly. I was not sure whether he was telling the truth at first. I kept an open mind.'

'I was only sixteen,' she cried mutedly, her green eyes blazing at him. 'How could you believe such a wicked lie!'

He smiled wryly. 'My dear young lady, age was nothing to do with it. Adolescent girls are notoriously provocative. It was possible he was telling the truth. That was all I needed to know. In order to represent my client adequately I had to destroy your evidence.'

'You nearly destroyed me,' she said bitterly.

Their whispered conversation was so intense, so emotional, that the other dancers were glancing at them curiously, and she felt her cheeks burn as suddenly she met Ashley's icy, watchful gaze from a few feet away. He was dancing with Renata again, their bodies moving in close harmony, but she guessed that he had been observing her and her partner for some time. Had he overheard their words? Did he know who Sir Daniel was? He had read a report of the trial, she remembered, and might recall Sir Daniel's name as defence counsel.

Looking down at her, Sir Daniel said gently, 'By the end of the trial I knew you were innocent, my dear. It was quite obvious to me, as it was to the jury.'

Selina looked back at him, her eyes filled with night-mare memories. 'Have you any idea what that did to me? Those staring eyes ... the curiosity ... the endless questions? I felt ...' Her voice broke off, shaking.

'As though I'd raped you publicly?' he asked quietly.

Hot colour ran into her face, and she stared up at him, starting. 'Yes,' she whispered hoarsely, trembling.

He had steered her to the edge of the dance floor. Now he put an anxious hand under her arm and helped her through a dim archway into a quiet corner of the lounge. Most of the guests were either dining or danc-ing. The lounge was empty. Sir Daniel gently pressed her into a corner of a couch in an alcove and sat down beside her, his thin hands resting on his knees.

Selina closed her eyes, leaning back against the leather upholstery. Her mind was in echoing confusion. After a while Sir Daniel's quiet presence was recalled to her and she opened her eyes to look at him. He was watching her carefully, his face concerned.

'I understand, you know,' he said, smiling slightly at her. 'Did you imagine yours was the first such case I had ever handled? Or the last, indeed? The reason I remember you is chiefly because of your extraordinary beauty, and your tragic circumstances ... your mother's death coming so soon after the trial, the way that beast had beaten both you and your brother.'

'He was vile,' she said hoarsely. 'Why did you take his case?'

He shrugged. 'I can't choose my clients on a personal basis. I dislike most of them, indeed. When I defend a murderer, do you think I do it because I like him, or necessarily believe in him?'

'Why do you defend such people?' she asked angrily.

'Because they have the same rights under the law as anybody else,' he told her calmly. 'They have to be defended. As my client's representative I am speaking on his behalf. I plead the case he wishes me to offer the court. If my client rejects my advice I am helpless, since I'm only his voice.'

'You make it sound very plausible,' she said, angry because he had impressed her with his argument when she had wanted to hate him as she had hated him for years.

He smiled at her, and she had the strangest sensation at that smile, as though he had the ability to read her mind and sense every tiny change of mood or feeling. He had such a quiet, restrained manner of speaking. It contrasted oddly with his cold, driving savagery in the courtroom. He was almost two separate, quite distinct personalities in one body. This gentle, civilised man— and the cruel, silver-tongued sadist who had whipped her with his tongue and left her defenceless and humiliated in front of a courtroom full of people.

'I've hated you for years,' she said abruptly.

The pale blue eyes showed no flicker of surprise. 'I imagined you would do,' he said softly. 'Your eyes were very revealing at the time. You make a good hater, Selina. I looked for you after the trial—I wanted to apologise.' He smiled oddly. 'It was the first time I'd ever been personally concerned in that way. I surprised myself. I found that your mother had died and you had vanished, taking your little brother with you. How did you manage to live? I worried about you for a long time.'

She sighed, her face filled with poignant thought. 'A friend helped us ... he owned a nightclub and he gave me a job.'

Sir Daniel's brows drew together in a forbidding line which was unpleasantly familiar. 'I see,' he said thinly.

Her green eyes mocked him. 'You're jumping to conclusions, Sir Daniel.'

For a moment his face was expressionless, then a charming smile suddenly warmed the cold, austere features. 'I'm very relieved to hear it, Selina. You see, remembering your circumstances and your amazing looks, I feared at the time that you might come to grief in a way I would have regretted very much.'

She was amused by his careful phrasing. 'You thought I'd become a scarlet woman, Sir Daniel?'

A flicker of amusement passed over his face. 'Something like that. What actually became of you?'

'I became a singer,' she said. 'But now I'm married.'

He leaned back, looking at her closely. 'Which of the two gentlemen you were with tonight is your husband?'

She lowered her eyes, her lashes sweeping her tender cheek. 'Guess, Sir Daniel,' she invited teasingly.

'I hope it's not the gentleman who could give me five years,' he said drily.

'It isn't,' she said, smiling at him through her lashes.

He leaned towards her, his eyes fixed on her face, a strange glinting light in the pale cold eyes. 'You're even lovelier than I remember,' he said, his beautiful voice like smoke, whispering insidiously. 'I've never been able to get your face out of my head, Selina. You've haunted me for years. I knew in my bones that one day you would walk back into my life. The only thing I regret is that it's taken so long ...'

A movement beside them broke them both out of the strange quivering trance which held them. Selina started, her slanting green eyes widening in shock.

Ashley was lounging there, his face enigmatic, the grey eyes riveted on her face in a probing disection of her feelings which she instinctively tried to elude by glancing down.

'If you're ready, Selina,' he said coldly, 'I think it's time we left. Come and say goodnight to our hosts.' The tone was so chilly that she felt like running away instead of standing up to face him, but she had no option but to obey.

'Won't you introduce me to your husband, Selina?' Sir Daniel asked courteously.

Staring at the floor she mumbled an introduction. 'Ashley, this is Sir Daniel Ravern. Sir Daniel, my husband, Ashley Dent.'

Sir Daniel's eyebrows lifted curiously. 'Ashley Dent?' The surprise in his voice made Ashley's hard mouth tighten. He held out his thin, finely shaped hand. Slowly Ashley extended his own, his manner unyielding. 'I've heard of you, of course, Mr Dent,' Sir Daniel said politely.

'And I've heard of you,' returned Ashley, making the statement sound like a deadly insult.

Sir Daniel glanced at Selina, one brow flickering in silent enquiry. She looked up, sensing his glance, and met his eyes without comment.

'I'm only here for a week,' Sir Daniel said coolly. 'It would give me great pleasure if you would lunch with me one day.'

Ashley's lips parted to show cruel white teeth. 'I'm

sure my wife would be delighted to renew the acquaintance, but I'm afraid our time is very limited. We're flying home very shortly.'

She looked at him in astonishment. He did not appear aware of her surprise, nor of her eyes on him.

Sir Daniel shrugged elegantly. His silvered fair hair was gleaming in the soft lighting, making him look younger than his actual years. He must be forty-five, Selina realised, if not more, but his lean frame and expensive, well-cut clothes disguised his age.

Ashley moved away, a brief peremptory gesture making it clear that he expected her to follow him. She sensed that he was so angry that he could not bear to touch her. Bending her head in weary resignation, she turned to go. Sir Daniel offered her his hand and after a faint hesitation she held out her own, and to her surprise and shock he lifted it to his mouth, kissing the back of her hand with a Gallic gesture which seemed entirely natural to him despite his austere appearance.

She shivered at the touch of the cool mouth, pulling her fingers away involuntarily, and their eyes met.

Then she followed Ashley like a sleepwalker. Mr Campbell and Renata were at their table. The blonde girl's avid, curious eyes observed Selina intently as she approached. Ashley made their farewell brief, his face and voice formally polite.

Selina dreaded the moment when they would be alone together. She knew he was going to ask questions and make cruel, biting comments. She could sense it from his withdrawn manner, and the prospect was unendurable. Sir Daniel's unexpected appearance had thrown her into turmoil. His deliberate, calculated attack on her in the courtroom had been a form of

intellectual assault she had not been capable of understanding or resisting at the time, but it had left her with
an indelible impression of him. She remembered reading that the victims of torture sometimes formed an
erotic secret relationship with their torturers, the more
potent for being buried in the mind. Her feelings towards the man whose cold, savage questions had de-
graded and insulted her had been complex at the time.
His face and voice had haunted her dreams for years.
She could not always remember her dreams on waking,
but she knew that the feeling in them had not been
entirely distasteful, and her angry reaction to her own
secret attraction towards him had been a purely conscious emotion. Beneath her conscious mind her unconscious had fostered quite different feelings.

She did not understand the twisted snake of her
emotions. She only knew that some hidden part of her
mind had responded treacherously to that penetrating
stare, those pale firm lips which could utter such cruel,
destructive words. She had hated him, as she told him.
But she had been deeply aware of him too, and she had
to resolve that residue of old pain before she could for
ever put her past behind her.

Ashley's silence as they drove back to the villa was
a relief. Selina had dreaded an outburst of jealous questions, but instead he drove in silence, staring at the
road, his face expressionless.

The villa was quiet and dark. Joanna would be at
home with Amos and her children, she reminded herself, as she followed Ashley into the building.

'I think I'll go straight to bed,' she said humbly,
pausing in the corridor outside the kitchen.

'I think not, my dear,' Ashley said tersely, his fingers

gripping her upper arm, making her wince. 'We have some talking to do, don't you agree?'

He switched on the light in the kitchen and propelled her into the room. She stood by the table, her head bent, in an attitude of feminine weakness, the slight body drooping, the hair tumbling across the pale fragile neck.

'Sir Daniel Ravern,' Ashley said, dropping the name syllable by syllable. 'You've never mentioned him to me before.'

'He defended my stepfather,' she said huskily.

'I'm aware of that. According to your testimony, and what I read in the newspaper, he crucified you in the witness box. Yet tonight you let him walk off with you without a protest. How much did you see of him all those years ago, Selina?'

She lifted her head wearily. 'Don't, Ashley!'

He moved closer, his eyes contemptuous. 'Don't what? Ask for the truth? I heard the last part of your intimate little tête-à-tête. When he was admitting that you'd haunted him for years, that he couldn't get you out of his mind ... what couldn't he forget, Selina? That he cross-examined you brutally? Surely not? There must have been some more intimate occasion to remember for him to be so obsessed by a sixteen-year-old girl.'

She looked at him with dislike and cold exhaustion. 'You wouldn't understand if I explained.'

'Try me,' he said hoarsely.

'No,' she said simply. 'I can't begin to make you understand.'

'Why not?' His voice was bitter.

'Because I don't understand myself,' she said.

He stared at her. 'You don't imagine I'm going to leave it at that?'

She turned away. 'You'll have to,' she said. 'I'm not talking about it any more. I've had enough for one night.'

For a moment Ashley stood quite still where he was, his face a mask of conflicting emotions, then he followed her down the corridor to her bedroom. Selina slipped inside and bolted the door. He banged on it with his fist, his voice burning with rage.

'Let me in, Selina, or I'll smash it down!'

'Do what you please,' she said indifferently, stripping off her clothes without taking any notice of the noise he was making, his hands pounding on the door.

She walked naked into the shower and turned it on, standing under it briefly, her flesh tingling under the cool water. Dripping, she took a towel and began to dry herself. Ashley had stopped banging on the door, she noted without interest. She picked up the filmy drift of her nightdress and dropped it over her head, then slid into bed. She was totally numb, uncaring about Ashley's whereabouts and feelings. She longed for sleep with an almost sensual desire. She wanted total unconsciousness, escape from herself and the tangled motives of her unwary emotions.

Her brain shut down completely. She relaxed, mindless and empty. And sleep came.

CHAPTER SEVEN

SHE slept until almost midday in a sleep which was close to coma, so deep that when she woke up at last her body was aching with the tension of long hours of immobility and dreams she could not recall in the daylight but which made her wince as she tried to remember them.

She showered again and dressed in white trousers and a low, sleeveless shirt. The villa was utterly silent. When she went into the kitchen it was spotless, but there was no sign of Joanna. Selina made herself some coffee, wondering where Ashley was, but feeling no impulse to look for him.

When his step sounded behind her she visibly jumped and her whole body stiffened as if in expectation of a blow.

'I'll have a cup of that coffee,' he said coolly, sitting down at the table.

She made no reply, but she poured him a cup and turned to give it to him.

His grey eyes ruthlessly searched her face, seeing the telltale pallor, the dark shadows under the green eyes, the trembling of the sweet, curved mouth.

As she placed the cup on the table his hand shot out to take her wrist and hold her, pulling her against his thigh. 'Now comes the reckoning,' he said menacingly. 'If you thought you would escape it by hiding in your room, you were mistaken.'

'I was asleep,' she said, angrily aware of pleasure in the hard muscled feel of his thigh against hers.

'Now you were going to explain about Sir Daniel Ravern to me,' he said tightly.

'I was not going to do anything of the kind,' she said, a hot flush staining her cheeks.

'I think you will,' he said between his teeth. 'Do I have have to beat it out of you?'

'Is force all men ever understand?' she cried angrily.

His grip tightened, wringing a low cry from her. 'I want to know, Selina,' he said. 'I intend to know. You might as well tell me at once. You ought to know that my tenacity usually gets me what I want in the end.'

'However low you have to stoop to achieve your ends,' she said scornfully.

His face darkened. 'Don't speak to me in that tone!'

'What do you expect? You're bullying me. Let go! You're hurting my wrist!'

For a moment he stared at her, a muscle jerking in his cheek. Then he flung her hand away with an angry, savage gesture.

Selina moved away and got her own cup of coffee, sat down and sipped it, her lids half closed.

Ashley swore under his breath. 'Why won't you tell me? Do you want me to put my own construction on the way you behaved last night?'

'You didn't exactly behave like an angel yourself,' she said.

'What's that supposed to mean?'

'You and Renata Campbell,' she flung, her green eyes rising to flash at him.

He was still, his glance intent. 'Ah, Renata,' he said softly. 'Lovely, isn't she? A golden rose.'

'And so easily plucked,' she said bitterly. 'Not a thorn in sight!'

He grinned, leaning back to survey her. 'Careful, my darling, you sound jealous again.'

'Isn't that exactly what you wanted?' she asked bitterly.

His eyes altered. A sweet, demanding smile came into them and her heart missed a beat.

'Are you admitting you were jealous?' he asked softly.

She made no reply, her eyes held by his, their expression only too revealing.

Ashley put down his cup and stood up, drawing her to her feet. His hands bore down on her, pressing her close against him, his hands warm and possessive against her back, their heat burning through the thin cotton shirt. She sighed, too weary to prolong a struggle, and submitted to his embrace, leaning her forehead on his shoulder.

After a moment he tangled a hand in the wild red-gold hair and pulled her head back firmly, exposing her face to his searching gaze.

'No fight left in you, my darling?' he asked unsteadily.

Submissively she lifted her mouth. He stared at her, trying to probe the secrets in the shadowed green eyes. She was softly yielding, her body passive against him, and a frown drew his brows together.

'Damn you,' he said raggedly. 'I don't want to make love to a doll. What are you thinking about?' Then, on a savage note of jealousy, 'Who are you thinking about?'

'I'm not thinking at all,' she said truthfully.

He swung her up into his arms. The dark face

glared down at her. 'Then I'll have to make you think,' he said tautly. 'And about me.'

He carried her into the bedroom and laid her on the bed, as he had the previous day, but this time Selina did not attempt to run away or struggle. Limply passive, she watched as he put his hands to her shirt and undid the buttons one by one, kissing her skin between each one. His hands slid under to unhook her bra, sliding it down over her naked shoulders, then she heard his breath catch and he laid his dark head against her breasts, his face turned to nuzzle their smooth whiteness.

'Your skin is so white there, against the tan of your shoulders and arms,' he said huskily. 'Selina, tell me you want me, tell me you belong to me ...'

She sighed wrenchingly. 'At the moment I want nothing but peace,' she said tremulously.

His angry muttered reply made her wince. He sat up and looked at her, pushing a hand through his black hair. His facial muscles were tense. The strong jaw was clenched as if to control some angry reaction.

'I thought I hated it when you fought me like a frightened animal,' he said. 'But this is worse ... for God's sake, what's wrong with you?' Then, inexorably, 'Is it Ravern? It is, isn't it? You changed totally when you saw him. You've been like this ever since. What was between you two?' He lifted her in his hands, shaking her vigorously, her red-gold hair tossing to and fro against her bare shoulders. 'Tell me, damn you! Tell me!'

'I don't know,' Selina whispered weakly.

He stopped shaking her, staring down into her eyes. 'Tell me the truth.'

'I am ... I don't know ... He was cruel to me and I hated him. But I've dreamt about him ever since. When I saw him last night it was like falling headlong back into a nightmare.'

He frowned, watching her. 'You find him attractive?' he asked coolly. 'Is that it?'

Hot colour ran up under her skin. 'I ... I don't know ...'

'There must be something,' he said. 'I could feel it between the two of you—an invisible thread between you.'

'There's something so ... personal ... about being cross-examined like that,' she whispered. 'It ... it's ...'

'Intimate?' he asked levelly.

She lowered her eyes, biting her lower lip, nodding slightly. When she glanced up, Ashley was watching her expressionlessly, his eyes unreadable.

'When you dreamt about him,' he said slowly, 'what exactly did you dream?'

She had to look away again, shaking her head mutely. His hand lifted her chin, holding her head so that she could not look away.

'You dreamt he made love to you?'

She gasped, shaking, 'No!'

His eyes cruelly observed her, his face like stone. 'Are you sure, Selina?' he asked in that level tone.

'I can't remember,' she admitted. 'They were terrifying dreams and I didn't want to remember them.'

He sat up, his face turned away from her. She lay back on the pillow, her eyes closed. Then his voice broke in upon her thoughts again.

'Tell me the truth. Did you ever confuse him with your stepfather, in these dreams? Was it sometimes him assaulting you?'

Selina moaned, her head turning from side to side in silent rejection of the idea. Ashley placed a hand on either side of her head and leant over her, his face close to her own, the grey eyes boring into her, reading her thoughts.

'I knew there was more to it than you were prepared to tell me,' he said carefully. 'Well, there's one way of driving him out of your head ...' His mouth came down hard, taking hers by storm, the sheer ruthless drive of his demand making her yield herself up, her lips parting helplessly. She gasped at the savagery with which he kissed her, but despite her weariness her body awoke from its dormancy and pulses began to beat like drums in her throat and wrists and body. His tongue tip touched her, moving insidiously along the dry line of her lips. Groaning, she let her hands move round him, her palms against his back.

Deftly he undid his own shirt and slid out of it. Selina lay with half closed lids, watching him submissively as he stripped. When he came back to her again it took him one minute to ignite the sensual hunger lying beneath the surface of her mind. His coaxing, seductive kiss deepened as she came to life under his expert hands, and their mouths moved closer in exchanged, equal passion.

As before, he began to cover her with those brief, light unsatisfying kisses, tormenting and arousing her, until she was frantic with pleasure, her slender nakedness on fire, the low groans she uttered sounding to her as if some other creature made them.

Then he raised himself above her, his face strangely pale, his eyes blazing with triumph. 'Say it now,' he demanded thickly.

She did not need to ask what he wished her to say.

Her tongue was already obeying him, moaning out her desire for him, murmuring his name passionately.

As he possessed her she caught her breath, then expelled it in a weak sob of sound which was more pleasure than pain. His mouth went on caressing hers, and gradually a bitter tension wound up inside her, tightening unbearably until she thought she would go mad if it did not stop.

Hardly knowing what she was saying, she told him she wanted him. 'I love you, I love you,' she whispered in a dry, scarcely audible voice throbbing with desire.

Her eyes were shut tight, her head thrown back in a gesture of intolerable excitement. She could feel the aching tension along her jaws and cheekbones, and when again he lifted his head to stare at her she knew what he saw; the unmistakable mask of total desire, unthinking, frenzied, feverish.

'Oh, God, you're so lovely,' he said hoarsely.

'Don't stop,' she begged, her mouth parted imploringly.

His lips moved down to take her mouth again, but even as his kiss deepened she felt the taut cord of her hunger snap, and she fell shuddering into an abyss of endless satisfaction, taking him with her. Against her mouth he groaned out her name again and again, his breathing rhythmic and quickening, his heart thudding against her as if he could scarcely control it.

The silence afterwards had the quality of a summer afternoon, warm, lazy and totally restful. Selina could feel every inch of her own body in a new way, conscious of muscle and skin, nerve and sinew. And most of all conscious of Ashley's relaxed and heavy nakedness against her, his face pillowed on the rise and fall of her breasts.

When at last he moved to sit up and look at her she was so shy she could not meet his gaze.

'Now tell me you don't want me,' he said, his tone unexpectedly savage.

She opened her eyes at that, frowning. Surely he knew now that she loved him? She had told him so again and again while he was making love to her. Why was he so angry?

The dark face was filled with brooding as she looked at it. 'All those years of frustration,' he said bleakly. 'Wanting you like hell and driven mad because I couldn't have you. I should have taken you mercilessly, but instead you kept me eating my heart out while you nursed your desire for revenge on the whole male sex.'

'Ashley,' she whispered, her eyes pleading with him.

His eyes were contemptuous. 'Well, now the tables are turned, my darling. You want me and I know it now. You're going to pay for every hour of misery you put me through. You're going to eat your heart out with frustration and desire. You'll have to learn to beg, Selina. I'll make you beg every time.'

'Don't!' she exclaimed, wincing at the look in his face, the sound of his voice.

'You stripped me of every ounce of pride, do you know that?' he asked hoarsely. 'For three years I had a private detective watching you. Can you imagine how that made me feel? If I'd had any pride left I would have put you out of my head and salved my hurt esteem with someone more available, but I couldn't even do that. No woman looked desirable to me. It had to be you or nothing. When you rejected me you made it impossible for me to forget you. You knew that very well. That was just what you wanted, wasn't it, my darling? It pleased you to think of me as consumed

with unsatisfied passion, didn't it? It was the revenge
you wanted.'

'No,' she whispered. 'No!' Her face was utterly
white, her eyes despairing. His words made it plain that,
desire her though he did, he also hated her.

'Oh, yes,' he said, the words grinding out between
his teeth. 'You enjoyed being the candle to my moth,
Selina. You liked watching me flame helplessly against
your brightness, unable to escape or get what I wanted.'

'Stop it, Ashley,' she moaned. 'How can you be so
cruel? When just now I ...'

'You finally surrendered?' His voice was icy. 'Has it
occurred to you yet, my darling, that that has set me
free?'

Her eyes stared at him, widening in pain and disbelief. 'What do you mean?'

'You understand me very well,' he said drily. 'I got
what I wanted in the end—I told you I always did.
You finally wanted me as much as I wanted you. Doesn't
it seem logical that having had you so satisfactorily I
should no longer want you?'

She closed her eyes to shut out the cruel mask of his
face. A swimming sensation was creeping over her body.
She gave a soft strangled moan and her limbs relaxed.

When she regained consciousness she was lying beneath a sheet, her cold body growing slightly warmer.
A movement beside her drew her dazed eyes. As she
saw Ashley she winced, her lips shaking.

'You'd better stay in bed all day,' he told her coolly.
'You're quite white. I've got to go into town to see the
Campbells. Joanna will come over to look after you.'

Selina made no movement, uttered no sound, her

eyes staring at him dully. He was a total stranger again, and she felt lost.

After waiting for some comment she never made, he shrugged. 'I'll see you later,' he said, moving out of the room.

She lay there staring at nothing, trying to drag herself out of the cold pit of despair. Then gradually anger grew steadily inside her. His bitter cruelty had come as such a shock after what had preceded it. She had to admit in all justice that her own treatment of him in the past might explain it, but she could not excuse it. Ashley had treated her like a woman of the streets, his attitude one of total hostility. He hated her. She had to face the fact. Her abject surrender had completed the alienation the past had begun. Between them they had destroyed their love for each other.

But what did he mean to do? He had not been very clear on the point. He had said that she would have to beg for his love at first, then he had said he didn't even want her any more. Which was the truth? Was their marriage at an end? Had he gone to Renata Campbell tonight? Was he going to leave her?

The golden afternoon sun flooded across the floor, so lyrically beautiful that it made her tears rise again.

The telephone began to shrill beyond her room. She heard Joanna answer it, the low murmur of her voice. Slipping out of bed, Selina put on her wrap and went out to see who was calling, hoping wildly that it would be Ashley.

Joanna was just replacing the receiver. She turned and looked surprised when she saw Selina standing there. 'Why, you're awake ... Mr Dent said you was goin' to sleep all day.' Her eyes twinkled. 'Honey, you must be tired out!'

Selina flushed at the amusement in the dark face. 'Who was that on the phone?' she asked anxiously. 'Was it A— my husband?'

'No, Mrs Dent, ma'am, it was a gentleman ... Sir Daniel something or other, he called himself. I told him you was not to be disturbed, just like Mr Dent said.'

'Oh!' Ashley had thought of everything, she thought bitterly. He might not want her any more, but he did not intend her to see or speak to Sir Daniel. That streak of possessiveness ran deep.

Joanna eyed her reflectively. 'You going back to bed, Mrs Dent?'

Selina shook her head. 'No, I'm going to get into my bikini and have a swim, I think.'

Joanna chewed her lower lip. 'Mind if I pop back home? I was in the middle of the ironing when Mr Dent asked me to come over, and if you're feeling better you may not be needing me.'

'That's all right, Joanna. I'll be fine by myself.' Selina said quietly. She went back into her bedroom and changed into her bikini, then wandered down to the beach and stared across the blue sea with eyes which contemplated an empty future. Kicking the fine soft sand with her bare toes, she stood at the water's edge, feeling the cool salty waves trickle over her feet. She was half tempted to walk out and never come back. Even in her worst moments she had never felt quite so desolate and lonely. She had always had Roger to worry about in the past. He had been the spar to which she clung in the shipwreck of her life. His need of her had kept her afloat. However sick and horrified she had been years ago she had known she had to look after him. and it had been his desperate need which had saved her from falling totally beyond hope. Now Roger was an adult and far away from her, and she had no living human being to care for, no one who needed or wanted her.

The blue sea stretched to the edge of the horizon, misty in its furthest reaches, with the late afternoon sun a blurred golden coin wrapped in opalescent wraiths of cloud. It was exquisite, but empty, and echoed her own feeling poignantly.

What was Ashley doing now? Making love to Renata Campbell? Teasing her, flirting with her, dancing with her?

She turned restlessly, to twist her mind away from such thoughts, and found herself under silent observation.

Sir Daniel Ravern stood a little way up the beach, looking curiously out of place in this setting, his light-weight dusty white suit flawlessly pressed, the creases knife-edged. The wind lifted his silvery fair hair with a caressing motion. His face was as austere and remote as the blue sea.

He moved down towards her slowly. 'I had the most curious feeling, while I watched you, Selina,' he said as he joined her. 'I got the idea you were thinking of killing yourself.'

It was typical of him that he should speak so bluntly. She smiled drily at him. 'I was,' she said, equally direct.

The cold eyes surveyed her again, very intently. 'Why?'

She shrugged, her slender shoulders lifted in a hopeless gesture. There was no point in trying to explain.

He glanced around the beach. 'A paradise,' he said. 'Where is the serpent, Eve? Is it myself?'

She couldn't help smiling, although the smile was weary. 'No, Sir Daniel. Don't ask me any more of your clever questions—please.'

'No cross-examinations?' His tone was as dry as her own. 'I rang you earlier, but your maid said you were asleep. But I saw your husband swimming in the hotel pool with Miss Campbell, so I deduced that that it would be quite safe for me to come out here to see you.'

'We have nothing to say to each other, Sir Daniel.'

'Possibly not,' he said in his beautiful clear voice. 'I think we had a time and place, but we missed it.'

Her eyes widened as she stared at him. What on earth did he mean?

His mouth twisted wryly. 'When you were sixteen I was thirty-six,' he said. 'I was on my way to getting my silk. I was a Q.C. when I was forty. I never had much time for women. Not that I didn't enjoy their company, or desire them occasionally, but I didn't wish to waste my energy in amatory pursuits when I had a career to build. I'm not trying to say I fell in love with you during those days in court, but I never quite got you out of my head. You had an unusual purity of feature, a vulnerability, which I found moving.'

She flushed. 'Thank you.' The dry tone with which he paid the compliment was touching.

'Had you been older, or I younger, I would have left no stone unturned to find you,' he said casually. 'As it was I was half grateful that you were lost to me. You would have been a distraction I couldn't afford.'

Selina laughed, her slanting green eyes filling with amusement. 'I think you mean it as a compliment!'

He smiled, the cold eyes lighting up. 'If you knew me better you would know I do. Anyway, the chance was lost. But now I want to tell you just one thing ... if you ever need me, come to me. You'll find my address in the telephone book. Don't be put off by my house-keeper. Leave your name and where I can find you. If I can ever be of any assistance whatever, I shall be very happy.'

'Thank you,' she said, indescribably touched now. She looked at his face curiously. 'What makes you think I may need such help?'

He looked away across the blue sea. 'The way you stood there just now, like a lost and desolate child ... and the way your husband spoke to you last night.' He held up one thin, finely shaped hand. 'Mind, I ask no questions. If you wish to confide in me, I shall listen, but I don't want you to think I'm prying, merely that I'm there if you should need me.'

She nodded, her red-gold hair blowing in the wind, unaware that her face had a soft sadness which made her look both vulnerable and lost.

Staring across the sea, she said huskily, 'I used to dream about you for years.'

He stood very still for a while. Then he said gently, 'That's quite a common experience, I'm told. Psychiatrists say that it's the unconscious mind attempting to make sense of an otherwise unacceptable experience.'

Selina turned her head in quick surprise, her hair blowing across his lips in a scented golden strand. 'You mean it happens to other people?'

He smiled. 'So I'm given to understand. It has the same sort of reasoning behind it as the transfer of affection to a doctor during the time he's treating a patient. The intimate relationship involved sets up a pseudo-sexual response. Patients and legal clients both tend to fall in love with the men they're dealing with.'

She laughed, flushing. 'I see.'

He smiled again, wryly. 'I'm being totally honest, against my own interests, Selina. I would like to let you imagine your dreams of me were unique and very real. I would like to believe you remember me as clearly and as pleasantly as I remember you. But honesty forces me to tell you the opposite. You were very young, your mind was still plastic. You received a distinct impression from me ... and it clung on, long after it would otherwise have faded. If you'd met me five years later in other circumstances it would probably have left you totally untouched.'

She smiled at him. 'You have such a clear, logical mind, Sir Daniel. Thank you.'

He grimaced. 'Please, don't thank me for anything. You've cost me a lot of sleepless nights. I bitterly regret having taken that case, never more so than now.'

She looked down. 'Thank you.' She looked at him from beneath her long lashes. 'If we're being honest, I must tell you that my dreams weren't pleasant.'

He looked at her shrewdly. 'Nightmares, you mean?'

'Sometimes.'

'And other times?'

Selina lifted her lashes slowly and the green eyes smiled at him. 'I think you've already guessed the answer to that.'

He flushed deeply and his face betrayed a sudden uncertainty. Then he moved away abruptly. 'Goodbye, Selina ... remember, if you need me, come to see me.'

'Goodbye, Sir Daniel,' she said gently, knowing she would never go to him.

He paused, looking back at her, his face slightly wistful. Then he came back, his skin reddened. He put a hand lightly under her chin, turning up her face, and bent forward. She did not move away. The kiss was gentle, undemanding, more of a farewell than a kiss of passion.

She watched him walk away up the beach, his shoes sliding on the fine sand. Then she turned and ran into the water and swam out into the blue, suntinted water, diving like a dolphin and turning head over heels, or drifting lazily in the warm and buoyant waves. The sun slowly sank beneath the horizon and with a rush it was dark. The fine steely tips of stars glittered in the purple mantle of the sky. Selina drifted about, her arms dabbling at the water, staring up at them, reluctant to go back into the villa. Out here she felt free of all the angry, tangled emotions of her life. She could stay out here for ever, she told herself. She would never come out of the sea.

If I were a mermaid, she told herself idly, I would comb my hair with a golden comb and sit on a rock luring sailors to their doom. Mermaids had no hearts. They could not feel as humans did. They just swam in and out with the tide, like living seaweed, experiencing life without being hurt, and their voices were unearthly and alluring.

Dimly at the back of her mind she knew she was acting foolishly. She felt delirious, as though she were touched by fever. Her thoughts wandered vaguely.

It hurt too much to think. This was much better, this lazy emptiness of mind and body. I've committed myself to the deep, she said aloud to the stars and the dark rolling waters, and laughed.

Then across the sea and the distant, pale sands came

Ashley's voice, filled with anger and panic and shaking anxiety.

'Selina ... Selina ... for God's sake!'

She could see him as the waves lifted her on a swell of warm water. He stood holding her towel in his hands, his white shirt a vague blur, staring out towards her. Then he threw down the towel and ran, shedding his clothes as he went.

She dimly heard the splash as he hit the sea. Her eyes had closed now and she was conscious of a growing desire to let herself sink down, down into the warm enveloping waves. Of my bones are coral made, she murmured through lips which felt swollen and shapeless.

Ashley's voice drifted to her again, but the ragged fear in his tones barely penetrated her tired brain. Salt was lapping gently at her lips. She made no attempt to swim towards him. In fact, she felt an angry resentment that he should disturb the soft shrouding peace which was engulfing her with his human panic and cries of pain.

When he reached her she was totally pliant, her eyes shut, the wet red-gold hair trailing on the water like some tropic weed.

Ashley took her round the shoulders and began to tow her towards the beach with an urgency which increased as he waded up the sand, dragging her, a dead weight, after him.

His violence brought her out of her safe trance, coughing and spluttering, salt water streamed out of her nostrils and mouth, painful, degrading, humiliating.

Weeping, she lay on her stomach, arms outstretched, as limp as a drowned doll.

Ashley lifted her into his arms, pushing back the sticky wet hair with an ungentle hand. His hand slapped her across her face hard and her eyes flew open. She moaned protestingly.

'Why ...'

His dark face bent over with hot flame sparking from his eyes. 'You little bitch, did you think I'd let you escape from me even in death? I would have followed you and found you even if I'd had to hunt you through the halls of hell. Do you understand?' His mouth violated her sore, salty lips, kissing her with a desperation which awoke her at last into a realisation of where they were and what had happened.

As he drew back his head she looked at him sadly, tears in her eyes. 'Don't hurt me any more, Ashley. Please, don't hurt me any more ...'

He looked at her in silence, his face white. Then with a sound like a moan he lifted her in his arms and began to walk up the beach with her clutched against his naked chest.

CHAPTER EIGHT

THE following morning she was up before the terrace was flooded with golden morning light. She had slept lightly, her mind unable to stop turning round and round within the confines of an inescapable future, seeking some way of escape. She could not bear the prospect of living with Ashley, knowing he hated her, yet she could not face the idea of leaving him again. She was chained, the prisoner of her love for him. Her only escape route had been tried, and she had failed. Ashley had closed that door to her in the future; she knew she would never again try to die in order to get away from him. There had been an element in his angry voice which had got home to her. His threat of following her even beyond death had made her shiver with fear, believing him. He had meant it. His desire for revenge was powerful enough to encompass his own death in order to punish her, and she knew she could never bear to think that she might be the cause of Ashley's death. She would have to stay here, bearing the full load of his hatred, and the realisation was terrifying.

She made herself coffee and found some fruit, sitting on the terrace in the first brightness of morning to stare out across the garden to the distant blue of the sea. The mist hung heavily out across the water, shimmering like shot silk, its pearly wreaths troubled by the blue and gold of the morning.

A white sail moved lazily out from the coast. Selina saw a boy moving on the deck, his orange life-jacket a splash of bright colour.

A footstep on the terrace floor made her stiffen, but she did not turn her head. Ashley sat down beside her, his eyes fixed on her clear profile.

'Good morning,' he said warily.

She turned her head then, her eyes veiled by her thick bright lashes. 'Good morning,' she said in a voice as cool as the morning mist.

His mouth tightened. 'How do you feel this morning?' The question was not idle, she could see that. Last night they had said nothing to each other after their return to the villa. He had carried her into her room, while Joanna clucked and exclaimed anxiously around them, and stood her on the carpet, shivering weakly, while Ashley stripped off her bikini, ignoring her faint moaned protest. His hands had been rough as he dried her thoroughly with a warm towel. Glancing at him just once she had seen his features taut with rage and had known that he kept his lips tightly shut to bite back what he wanted to say to her. He had dropped her nightdress over her head and pushed her into bed, drawing a warm coverlet over her still shivering body. Then he had left the room without a backward glance. Joanna had tiptoed in with a cup of hot milk five minutes later. Selina knew Ashley had ordered it for her, just as she knew who had told Joanna to bring her two aspirin to take with it. Obedient as a child, she had taken the pills and drunk the milk. Then she had lain in the darkness wishing she had died out in the warm, soothing sea.

Now she said to him quietly, 'I'm fine, Ashley.'

His eyes probed her face, trying to find some chink in the defences she erected against him.

She was very pale, and there were shadows under the green eyes, but her expression was calm and remote.

As if the remoteness angered him, he said bitingly, 'Well, that's reassuring. You tried to kill yourself last night, but this morning you're fine! Have you any idea how I felt, coming back to find you missing, and Joanna totally unaware of your whereabouts?'

'She knew I'd gone down to the beach,' she protested.

'Oh, she knew that—hours before, she told me. She'd just gone off home and left you there, despite my instructions to her to keep an eye on you!'

'It wasn't Joanna's fault,' she interrupted. 'She had no idea ...'

'No,' he jumped in tightly, 'how could she suspect

that a girl who was on her honeymoon might try such a stupid, cowardly trick?'

Selina flushed at that, her eyes dropping to the table. 'I'm sorry . . .'

'Sorry?' The fury in his voice was like a whiplash. 'You're sorry, are you? You're going to be a great deal sorrier, believe me!'

'Something else for you to add to your long list of grievances against me, Ashley?' she said bitterly.

He drew a shaky breath. 'I ought to wring your neck!'

'Why don't you?' Her eyes flew upwards to defy him. 'It would save us both a lot of trouble.'

His grey eyes savaged her, his lips drawn back from his teeth. 'I can think of more satisfactory ways of punishing you,' he said tightly.

'Why didn't you leave me out there?' she demanded raggedly. 'Why force me to come back to this?'

'Because you aren't wriggling out of things that easily, my darling,' he said, his voice biting. 'I want you under my eyes.'

'So you can watch me suffer, Ashley?'

'That's right,' he snapped. 'I want to see you trapped in the same hell you consigned me to for three years!'

'And after three years do I get a parole?' she asked him with a cold smile.

His hand snaked out to catch her by the upper arm, his finger tips digging into her so hard she knew she would have bruises there next day. 'No parole,' he said between his teeth. 'The sentence is life, Selina.'

She swayed, her face quite white, and stood up. Ashley rose with her, still holding her, his eyes fixed on her face.

'What was Ravern doing here last night?' he demanded after a moment.

She blinked, looking up at him through her lashes. 'Daniel?'

His mouth hardened. 'Oh, we reached Christian names last night, did we?'

She shrugged indifferently. 'He came to tell me something.'

'What?'

'That if I ever needed him I only had to ask,' she said, knowing perfectly well that it would infuriate him, and not caring.

'Was that before or after he kissed you?' Ashley demanded.

Her pallor was lost in a wash of bright pink. She looked at him, her eyes wide in surprise. 'How ...'

'Amos told me,' he said grimly. 'He saw you on the beach with a man. When I got back and started looking for you, Amos mentioned having seen you. His description fitted Ravern to a T.' His smile was unpleasant. 'It was charming to be informed by Amos that my wife had been making love on the beach with a complete stranger!'

She sighed, 'Amos exaggerated. Sir Daniel kissed me very lightly, just once ... a brotherly kiss. You wouldn't have objected if you'd been there.'

'Do you want to bet?'

'Dog in the manger, Ashley?' she asked lightly, trying to get the discussion back off what she felt to be dangerous ground.

His rage was terrifying. He shook her angrily, his hands on her slender shoulders. 'You belong to me. No other man is ever to touch you again. And you needn't consider Ravern's suggestion ... if you run away to him I'll find you if I have to tear London apart. There's nowhere in this world you can hide from me, Selina.'

'All this for revenge?' she asked, watching him through her lashes.

'That's right,' he said flatly. 'I want to watch you living with the knowledge that you can't have what you want ... and you do want me, Selina, we both know that, don't we? I want to see you go insane with frustration, as I did. You're going to think about me night and day until you're frantic.' His hands drew her nearer, and she tensed, unable to resist her own desire for the touch of his body against her. As she helplessly lifted her head his mouth lowered. A long sigh of hunger drifted from her parting lips. His mouth poised above hers, he watched her relentlessly, his eyes feverbright.

Slowly his mouth came down. Her lids fell. Her arms curved round his neck and she whispered his name. 'Darling, oh, darling ...'

The fleeting brush of his kiss sent fever burning along her veins. She stood on tiptoe to pull him back towards her, curving herself against him, breathing so fast her face became suffused with colour.

But he withdrew inexorably, and when at last she opened her eyes in a chill of disappointment, his smile was cruelly triumphant.

'You see what I mean?' he mocked. He took her hands and unwound them from their clinging grasp of his neck, pushing her away. 'Go and change into your bikini,' he commanded. 'We're going on the beach.'

In her bedroom she wept, crouched on the bed. At last she washed her face and changed into her bikini, then went out to join Ashley. He had changed too, and was wearing his swimming trunks. She could not avoid a swift, desirous glance at the hard brown body walking beside her, even though she knew that, with his sixth sense where she was concerned, he was at once aware of her feelings, and mocking them silently with his sidelong glance.

They sunbathed and ate, swam and rested in the garden, for the rest of their honeymoon. The long, sunny days were not so hard to take, Selina thought, but the warm tropical nights were unbearable. She tossed restlessly in her bed, unable to stop thinking about Ashley, and dark shadows deepened under her eyes. Each morning he would inspect her face with those merciless cold eyes, as if each new shadow on her skin were welcome to him.

Although she tried to keep away from him there were unavoidable moments of bodily contact, and she knew that each time her tense awareness was perfectly comprehended by him, and pleased him. He would give her a brief mocking look, his dark brows lifting in silent comment.

Once he forced her to dance with him after dinner, her slender body held tightly against him in a contact half heavenly, half intolerable. Deliberately his hand moved over her back and she could not repress a trembling sigh of pleasure. She felt his mouth harden into that cruel, pointed smile, and drew away from him at once, only to be pulled back without a word, her body yielding to the hard pressure of his hand.

The days seemed endless to her. She could not wait for the holiday to end. Beautiful, paradisal though this place was she would always remember it with pain.

On their last evening Ashley again demanded that she dance with him after dinner. Joanna had gone and the silence in the villa was eating at Selina's nervous awareness of him. They circled to the music in silence, her head close to his shoulder, her cheek almost touching his shirt. She could feel the warmth of his skin through the thin material and a sudden desperate desire to press her open mouth against him grew in her, making her stumble over his feet.

'What's wrong?' he asked mockingly, looking down at her.

'I must be tired,' she stammered. 'I think I'll go to bed.'

'I don't think so,' he said indifferently. 'I want you to dance with me.'

'For God's sake, Ashley,' she burst out, then stopped, seeing the sardonic light in his eyes sparkle at her.

Stiffening, she pulled out of his arms and moved towards the door, but he was behind her before she got far, his grip commanding. Pulling her back against him, he lowered his cheek against hers, his lips softly brushing her ear. 'What do you want, Selina? Say it!' Despite her struggle, he turned her round to face him, his hands slowly stroking her back and waist until she was too weak to protest. He lifted her chin with one hand, smiling coldly at her. 'Is this what you want?' he asked, his mouth moving nearer.

'Yes,' she moaned, her eyes unable to move from the hard, firm outline of his lips, the implicit sexual promise of their touch so close at last.

This time the kiss was not a brief, tantalising touch. His mouth possessed her, sending her up in flames, and she groaned, holding the back of his head to keep him there, her response an abject and adoring surrender.

Suddenly he pulled away, his face dark red, his

breathing so uneven that she knew she had not imagined the way his heart had begun to race against her
as the kiss deepened.

He looked at her savagely, his mouth snarling without a word, then turned and left the room.

Selina stood there, shaking, with a deep sense of satisfaction growing inside her. Ashley might hate her, but
his desire for her had not vanished, despite what he
said; that much she knew for certain now. She suspected
he had not meant to kiss her like that. He had been
carried away by his own emotions. The realisation was
comforting, giving her a new hope for the future which
carried her buoyantly through the remaining hours at
the villa.

Selina was sorry to say goodbye to Joanna, who had
become something of a friend during the last few days,
but she had brought her a present on their final visit to
the town—a gay yellow silk scarf which Joanna seemed
very pleased with when Selina gave it to her.

The flight back to London was quiet. Ashley seemed
absorbed in his own thoughts, hardly aware of her. She
flipped through the magazines he had bought her and
stared out of the window at the clouds through which
they flew before soaring up into the bright blue level
above them.

London looked grey and chilly. It was raining as they
drove through the crowded streets. Selina shivered in
her lightweight coat, remembering the halcyon blue of
the island with regret.

Ashley's flat was a penthouse overlooking one of the
royal parks. He stood in the teak-floored drawing-room,
swinging the key round on his brown finger, watching
her as she looked shyly around the room.

'I thought we'd eat out tonight,' he said abruptly. 'But this afternoon I must call at the office to see what mail is waiting for me. I'll only be gone for a few hours. Can you amuse yourself here while I'm away?'

'I could go shopping,' she said. 'I need a few small things.'

'No.' His dissent was categoric. 'Stay here.'

Her eyes lifted angrily to his face. 'Am I a prisoner, Ashley?'

His mouth moved in a taut smile. 'Yes,' he said. 'I can't trust you out of my sight. Don't try to leave, because Stow will have orders to stop you.'

Stow had been hovering in the wide hall when they arrived. A large bald man with a shuttered face, he had inspected Selina briefly as he was introduced to her. Her offered hand had been ignored, making her feel foolish. Ashley had described him as his 'Jack of all trades': butler, chauffeur, valet, handyman, willing to turn his hand to anything that offered.

'So Stow is my jailer?' she asked him now.

'You've hit the nail on the head,' Ashley retorted coolly.

'Are you sure you can trust him with me?' she asked sweetly.

Ashley's hard flush showed that she had hit her target, but the dangerous look of the grey eyes made her wish she had held her tongue.

'Stow dislikes women,' he said bitingly. 'I shouldn't try your charms on him, Selina. He's immune.'

'Like master, like servant?' she muttered.

His fingers bit into her soft chin, raising her head. 'Are you trying to provoke me, my darling?' he asked silkily.

Her tongue tip caressed her dry lips. 'Would I dare?' she asked, aware of the way he watched her slight movement.

'Don't do that,' he said with sudden harshness.

She knew in every nerve of her body that he wanted to kiss her, to lay his mouth along the line recently touched by her tongue. Her heart began to race and she lifted her eyes to his face, probing his expression.

He pushed her away and turned towards the door. 'I'll be gone for two hours or so,' he said flatly, slamming out of the room.

She began to explore the flat, enchanted by the panoramic view and the warmth and light which filtered through the wide windows. There were three bedrooms, all of them spacious and beautifully furnished in a modern Scandinavian style, with light, polished woods and discreetly shaded curtains and carpets. In the kitchen she found Stow moving about with a large blue and white striped apron shrouding his portly form. He looked at her expressionlessly as she entered the room.

'Can I help you, Mrs Dent?' His voice was calm, polite and utterly indifferent.

She had no intention of testing out Ashley's statement that Stow would stop her from leaving the flat. She did not want to bring a stranger into their armed struggle.

'I was just exploring,' she explained. She looked around the kitchen with delight. 'What a beautifully equipped room! What's that? An oven?'

'Yes, madam,' Stow nodded. 'Micro-wave.'

'Good heavens! They're supposed to cook things very quickly, aren't they?'

He nodded again. 'Very useful for heating frozen food,' he said.

Selina prowled around, looking at the large dishwasher, the deep-freeze cabinet which took up one corner, the washing machine and electric press and all the other expensive and elaborate machinery which had been installed.

'It must make it easy to run the flat,' she commented, thinking that she could do Stow's work herself.

As if he had read her thoughts Stow's face closed up. 'Yes, madam,' he said succinctly.

'You keep it looking very spick and span,' she offered, hoping to propitiate him.

'Thank you, madam,' he said politely and with utter coldness.

She opened a cupboard and glanced at the contents, then turned to look at him appealingly. 'Are you very busy, Stow?'

'I am preparing the dinner, madam,' he returned evenly.

'Oh!' She looked at him in surprise. 'Mr Dent said something about going out tonight.'

Stow's face stiffened. 'Indeed, madam? He did not mention that to me. I have cooked coq au vin. I was just about to prepare the lemon mousse to follow it ...' The cool voice was faintly touched with distinct irritation.

'Oh, what a pity,' she said softly. 'I love mousse ... I wonder if I can persuade him to change his mind and stay in after all? The flight was rather tiring and I would prefer to eat at home.'

Stow looked at her briefly, his fish-like eyes almost human. 'Would you like a cup of tea, madam?'

'Oh, thank you, Stow, that would be lovely,' she said warmly.

He coughed and looked away, apparently taken aback by the smile she gave him. 'I—er—have some chocolate cake, if you would care for a slice, madam.'

'Home-made, Stow?' she asked eagerly.

'I made it myself, madam,' he admitted.

'I'd love some,' she said. 'I adore chocolate cake, but somehow I can never get the chocolate icing to be as smooth as it should be.'

'I use melted chocolate, madam,' he said, producing a superb layered cake from a cupboard with the flourish of a conjuror who knows his tricks are amazing.

'That's the most marvellous cake I've ever seen,' she gasped, staring at it in genuine admiration.

He turned away to put the plug of the electric kettle into a socket. 'Tea will be about ten minutes, madam,' he said. 'I will serve it in the drawing-room.'

She knew it was dismissal, courteous but firm, and retreated obediently.

It was hours since she had eaten her light, rather plastic airport lunch, and she was ravenous, particularly since the cold weather of wintry London and her emotional energy drain had made her appetite keener.

When Stow appeared with a light table and laid it expertly with an embroidered cloth, the tea tray and a slim vase containing one hothouse rosebud, Selina sighed appreciatively. He left her sitting beside the electric log fire, nibbling at a large slice of his chocolate cake.

Half an hour later he reappeared to remove the tea things, and she congratulated him again on his cake. The fact that she had eaten two slices of it made his eyes soften and a smile of gratification appear on the usually stony face.

'I hope you will be able to eat your dinner, madam,' was all he said, however.

Teasingly she asked, 'Are you very politely telling me that I'm a pig, Stow?'

His face broke into an unguarded smile and he looked at her with a new look in his eyes. 'I would not be so presumptuous, madam,' he told her with quiet humour.

She laughed, the sound a lovely lilting echo in the quiet flat, and at that moment Ashley appeared in the door, having returned and let himself in without a sound.

Stow gathered together his discarded dignity and left, removing the tea things deftly.

Ashley leaned in the doorway, staring at her, his frown black. 'My God, even Stow isn't safe with you!' he breathed. 'I've never seen him smile like that in my life.'

She stood up. 'Stow is human, like the rest of us,' she told him lightly.

Walking towards him, she paused to wait for him to move aside. 'I want to dress for dinner,' she said. 'By the way, we can't go out—Stow has prepared the dinner. You forgot to tell him your plans and he'd worked hard getting a special meal for us.'

His mouth worked in silent rage, then he said bitterly, 'So you were sweetly sympathetic and made him your slave for life, I suppose? God, I should have known you'd find a way to reach him. You're as insidious as bindweed, aren't you, Selina?'

'May I go to my room?' she asked quietly.

Without a word he stood aside and she went past him. In her bedroom she checked through her clothes to find something new to wear. He had seen most of her dresses and tonight she wanted to wear something special.

Her hand halted on the last hanger. A frown touched the smooth surface of her forehead. She stared at the black silk dress hanging there, nervously biting her lip.

Dare she? She had never worn it privately before. It was strictly a stage costume, intended for public consumption at a great distance.

The revealing style and the smooth clinging material made it a dress which needed great daring to wear. Remembering the way Ashley had looked at her when she wore it on the first evening, when he came to the club after she had heard the false news of his death, she was both tempted and alarmed by the idea of wearing it tonight.

She showered, changed her underwear and used some of the ultra-expensive French perfume Ashley had given her during their honeymoon, then stood locked in mental argument with herself for a few moments before she took it down from the hanger.

She lingered over the last details of her make-up, too nervous to go out and join him, and eventually heard the door open behind her and his voice irritably demanding, 'Selina, why the hell are you taking so long?'

His glance flashed across the room and she saw his face for a second before a shutter came down and he controlled his expression.

'Well, well, well,' he said smoothly. 'Is this a declaration of war, Selina?'

His quickness made her flush revealingly. 'I thought

you liked this dress,' she said, pretending not to understand his meaning.

He smiled mockingly. 'What a very obvious and predictable little bitch you are, my darling.' He shrugged carelessly. 'But if that's how you want to play it, by all means go ahead ... it will be an amusing evening.' He pushed open the door behind him and waved a hand through the opening. 'Shall we eat this delectable meal Stow has dreamed up for us first, though? After all, you'll find your game easier to play if I'm softened up by wine and good food first.'

His mockery stiffened her backbone. She gave him a smile as bright and careless as his own, sweeping past him, her black silk skirts rustling.

Stow hovered behind her chair in the dining-room, watching anxiously as she tasted her chicken, relaxing when the red-gold head turned with a flicker of gleaming curls to smile at him. 'It's delicious, Stow.'

Ashley watched them with an ironic smile. 'Stow has always felt that I don't appreciate his skill as a chef,' he drawled.

Stow straightened reprovingly. 'Will you need me any longer, sir?' he asked, his face blank.

'No, thank you, Stow,' said Ashley. 'We'll help ourselves to what we want.'

Stow withdrew, closing the door behind him. Selina felt her nerves tighten, but she concentrated on her food without a glance at Ashley.

As she leaned forward later to spoon some of Stow's light-as-a-feather lemon mousse on to her plate she felt Ashley's brief, involuntary glance at the whiteness of her breasts above the black silk, and her pulses raced.

Coming into the room five minutes later with Brie

and a plate of biscuits, Stow quickly inspected the re-
mains of the mousse with a passing gleam of satisfaction.

'I hope everything was satisfactory, madam,' he said,
placing the cheese in the centre of the table. 'More
wine?'

'Thank you, Stow,' she nodded, and smiled round at
him. 'The mousse floated on my spoon. I've eaten far
too much, but it was worth it!'

Ashley made an irritable noise at the back of his
throat. 'Do you want some Brie, Selina?'

'No, thank you,' she said lightly, sipping her wine.
She had drunk enough to make her careless of consequences, and she had noticed with some satisfaction
that Ashley had drunk even more. His eyes were bright
and hard across the table as he looked at her.

Stow trod quietly from the room, only to come back
to announce that he had served the coffee in the
drawing-room.

'Which means you want us to get out of here, I suppose?' Ashley said grimly, rising from his chair.

'Stow wants to clear and wash up before he goes to
bed,' Selina pointed out, smiling at Stow gently.

'I'm aware of that!' Ashley had a belligerent note in
his voice as he took her elbow with fingers that bit into
her flesh.

The drawing-room was dimly lit by one table lamp
beside the fireplace. The log fire glowed with artificial
brightness. Stow had placed the small tea table beside
the couch and the coffee things were laid out there.
Sinking down on the couch with a swish of silk, Selina
poured two cups of coffee, added cream and handed one
to Ashley, who had taken up a brooding position in

front of the fire, his arm propped on the mantelshelf.

She sipped her coffee, one hand tucking back a stray lock of glittering hair. Ashley's eyes followed the movement with an intensity she could feel in every nerve.

'What do you intend me to do with myself, Ashley?' she asked. 'Stow obviously needs no help. You said you don't want me to work. What am I supposed to do all day?'

'The summer's flower is to the summer sweet,' he intoned mockingly. 'Though to itself it only live and die.'

Shakespeare, she noted vaguely, realising that Ashley was slightly drunk, his voice thickened by wine.

'That's hardly much help,' she protested. 'I must have some occupation, mustn't I?'

'You can sit on a cushion and sew a fine seam,' he said mockingly.

'Be serious, Ashley!'

'Oh, you'd like that, wouldn't you?' His eyes were dangerous as they stared at her. 'Too bad. I'm not playing your game, my devious darling. You'll have to do better than that.'

She glanced down, her lashes fluttering against the pale gold of her skin. 'You're drunk,' she said softly.

'Not drunk enough,' he retorted. 'I'm still firmly in control of myself, Selina—I warn you.'

She finished her coffee, feeling suddenly chilled, and stood up, her movement graceful in the close-clinging black silk.

Ashley's cup crashed down on the table and he was on his feet, too, his hand catching at her arm. 'Where the hell do you think you're going?'

'To bed,' she said quietly. 'I'm tired.'

His face worked in confused anger. 'Sit down again,'

he snapped, pushing her backwards. 'You'll go to bed when I tell you to and not before.'

She sat down, her face flushed with anger. 'Stop treating me like a slave, Ashley!' she exclaimed furiously.

He leaned over her, his eyes on her mouth. 'That's what you are, my darling. Haven't you realised that yet? I bought you. I can do what I like with you.'

She was very still, looking up at his dark features through the fine curtain of her lashes. 'What do you want to do with me?' she asked in pointed softness.

Dark red washed up his face. He drew back, his breath coming faster. Shoving his hands in his pockets, he moved back to the fireplace and leaned there, staring at her insolently.

'Pour me some more coffee.' The tone was hard and insulting. After a pause in which their eyes fought silently Selina bent her head in mute defeat and poured him some coffee. He made a curt gesture. 'Bring it to me.'

Her lips tightened, but she obeyed, offering him the cup. He stared at her as he accepted it. 'That's better,' he said in triumph. 'Now you see what sort of wife I want ... obedient, meek, submissive.' His voice taunted her lightly and she stared back at him, feeling she would like to slap his smiling face. Instead she moved back to her own seat on the couch without a word and poured herself some more coffee. They sipped their drinks in silence. She stared down into her cup, her retina imprinted with the image of Ashley's good looks, seeing him everywhere.

Her mind seemed powerless to fight the nagging hunger below the surface of her calm exterior. She wanted him. Sooner or later he would succeed in getting her to admit it openly, to do just what he wanted her to do, to beg for his kiss, his touch, his lovemaking.

When Ashley put down his cup and moved away from her she thought he was going to bed, and her eyes followed him in hopeless longing. But instead he moved to a long cabinet and bent to select a record from those housed inside. She watched him, placing her own cup down. A gentle whisper of music issued from the cabinet. He turned it up, then swung on his heel to hold out his hand to her.

Folding her hands in her lap, she said defiantly, 'I don't want to dance.' Not held in his arms, desperately conscious of his thighs moving against her and the power of that lean chest. She knew she could not bear that sort of proximity for long. He knew it, too. He knew it would provide the spark necessary to fuel her smouldering need of him. They were each playing a dangerous game, walking a tightrope over an abyss, and Ashley meant to make sure she fell first.

'Come here,' he commanded, his face hardening.

'No,' she denied him, shaking her head.

'If you make me come over there for you, you'll be sorry,' he promised silkily, and the strong hand beckoned her again.

Reluctantly she got up and joined him. His hand slid round her waist. The long fingers touched the naked flesh of her back and she felt them tremble, but when she looked up quickly Ashley's face was guarded against her, his features tautly controlled.

She moved closer. Fire fights fire, she told herself, pressing herself nearer, her hand flat against his shoulder. They began to circle the room. His cheek lowered suddenly to brush against hers, and she was tempted to turn her mouth just the little way needed to touch the hard brown cheek. He spun her round deftly to retrace their steps, and in the process her silk-clad thigh slid against his and she felt his sharp intake of breath. Deliberately she turned her face and her mouth touched his cheek.

With a savage movement he halted and caught her up against him with both arms tight around her slenderness, staring down into her uplifted face with eyes that ate her.

'I hate you,' he whispered hoarsely. 'I hate you so much I'm going insane ... kiss me ...' As he spoke the last words on a groan he brought his mouth down on her hard, burning with a fever the soft parting of her lips could not soothe, his hands touching her bare back with a desperation he had ceased to disguise.

The long insistent kiss drugged her into total submission. Her eyes closed tightly to shut out his demanding face and she gave up trying to think, sinking herself into a flood of sensual feeling.

When he pulled his head back she was still clinging to him, her hands tight against his neck, her face uplifted, the white lids closed over the green eyes, the soft mouth parted and swollen with passion.

The smothering silence broke in upon her and she raised her lids to look at him. He was watching her, his face tortured.

'You go to my head faster than wine,' he said in an attempt to speak lightly. 'I can't keep my hands off you.'

'Perhaps we'd better dance again,' Selina suggested.

His hands dropped and he stood back, shaking his head. 'No,' he said harshly.

She moved away slowly, the black silk rippling over the slender curves of her body. His eyes followed the movement with open desire. She moved to the door and halted, looking back at him with a sweet, unconscious invitation.

'I'm going to bed, Ashley. Goodnight.'

He neither moved nor said anything, and after a pause she went out. In her bedroom she shed her dress and got ready for bed. The room was furnished in luxurious style. The thick cream carpet seemed to engulf her bare feet as she walked to and fro, and her eyes admired the cream and gold of the bed, the matching furniture which was fitted into one side of the room.

She had her green, lacy nightdress in her hand when the door opened. Blushing hotly, she held it against her nakedness in a gesture of shy dismay.

Ashley was wearing pyjama trousers and nothing else. His face was a frozen mask as he moved swiftly towards her, snatching the nightdress away from her. 'You won't need that,' he said thickly.

Selina quivered, trying to read the look in the narrowed grey eyes.

For a full moment Ashley did not touch her, his eyes moving slowly over the warm golden skin of her shoulders, the emphasised whiteness of her breasts with their hard pink nipples encircled by a faint dark aura, down the taut, flat stomach to her brown hips and tapering thighs. She did not attempt to turn away, bearing the crucifixion of his stare as bravely as she could, deliberately keeping her eyes riveted on his face so that she would not look at his bare chest.

At last his mouth parted and he gave a harsh moan of

aching desire. 'You know perfectly well what you do to me, don't you, Selina? I said you were my prisoner. The truth is I'm yours—I have been for years. Years of wanting you and going without you. Years of obsessive, driving hunger which you would never satisfy. I want you so much I could break you in pieces. Hatred is a mild word for what I feel about you, Selina.'

'It was your decision not to make love to me any more,' she pointed out softly.

His teeth snapped together ragingly. 'Don't torment me! You know why I'm here.'

'Do I?' she asked whisperingly. 'Do I, Ashley?'

His hands descended, feverishly touching her, pulling her against him so that her breasts were crushed against the hardness of his chest. His kiss sent white-hot flame along her limbs, consuming them both. She lost all sense of time, her lips clinging in total response, her hands stealing round his waist to caress the bare brown back, making their own sensuous pilgrimage along the taut paths of his body until they buried themselves in his dark hair, twining among the thick strands.

Without removing his lips from hers, he lifted her and carried her to the bed, lowering her on to it before he slid down beside her, his kiss still burning along her mouth as though he could not bring himself to stop kissing her.

'Put out the light,' Selina whispered against his kiss, her heart thudding against her breastbone.

'No,' he refused harshly. 'I want to watch you.'

Some lingering cruelty in his voice made her moan in protest, pulling away from him.

As if inflamed by her denial, he knelt over her, pinioning her below him, with his hands crushing her face between their palms. His eyes flared, glittering at her like the points of knives. She saw no tenderness, no love in his face.

'Do you know what I planned should happen to-night?' he demanded. 'I meant to torment you until you were out of your mind. I wanted to see you lost to everything but your need of me.' His mouth twisted. 'Did you think I didn't know you were trying to seduce me by wearing that damned dress? You were too obvious, my darling. I told you it was war, didn't I?'

'It doesn't have to be,' she whispered, her eyes pleading with him.

'It does if I'm to regain my self-respect,' he said bitterly. 'I've danced to your tune long enough. Now you'll dance to mine. I want to hear you beg, Selina—nothing less will satisfy me. I've waited years for this and even though it would be damnably easy to let myself take you when you're lying there begging me with every look of those green eyes, I'm not going to touch you.'

'Darling,' she whispered again, her hands running up his chest to grip his shoulders. 'Kiss me.'

'Like this?' he asked thickly, bending forward until their lips met.

Selina moaned in satisfaction, throwing her hands up to touch his hair, but even as her mouth parted hungrily beneath his he drew away. Cloudy-eyed, breathing fast, she looked up at him.

'Yes, it's agony, isn't it? Sheer bloody hell.' His voice was harsh with mockery. 'Go on, my darling, show me how much you want me. I want the satisfaction of hearing you beg as I've begged so many times.'

For a second she was pierced with anguish, but her

senses were telling her something Ashley did not want
her to know. Even as he spoke so savagely his heart was
racing so fast it seemed impossible for it to go on beating, and although his smile taunted her, his eyes flamed
with a naked hunger which made her heart race.

'Do you know what you did to me?' he asked bitterly.
'You bloody well emasculated me. I destroyed my man-
hood over you. I threw away my pride, my self-control.
I despised myself, and I hated you for the way you made
me feel ...'

She saw now that in order to reach him she had to
restore his damaged pride. The long-delayed surrender
had driven him almost out of his mind. Torn between
love and hatred, they would never be able to reach
serene waters until Ashley's pride had been soothed.
He needed his revenge on her. He needed to see her
suffer as he had suffered in the past; nothing less would
do. Somehow she had to convince him she wanted him.
She had to abandon her own pride for him. He had to
be shown that her desire beat as hotly as his own, that
he could move her as strongly as she moved him.

She looked up at him through her lashes, seeing the
restless, barely controlled passion in his eyes, then she
raised her body until her mouth touched his shoulder,
her lips burning against his skin, her hands running
down his back in a slow caressing movement which
made the muscles ripple under her fingertips.

'I want you,' she whispered, burying her face in his
neck, feeling the pulse beating hard in the strong brown
column under her mouth. 'Take me ... make love to
me ... Ashley, I love you.'

He resisted her, his muscles tightening against her
silken seduction, but she clung to him, winding herself

against him, whispering soft invitation, melting in endless insidious kisses.

'Please,' she begged. 'Please, Ashley!'

She heard his groan of capitulation with a sensation of triumph which faded from her mind as he forced her back against the pillows. In the instant of possession her body seemed to turn to molten fire beneath him. There was no gentleness in their lovemaking, and Selina asked for none. He demanded and she gave, their bodies a mutual flame of undiminishing, desperate hunger which grew with every driving movement until it scorched along their flesh, consuming them.

When she was able to breathe again Ashley moved lazily against her, turning his head to gaze into her eyes. They were half closed in limp surrender, her lashes flickering on her cheek.

'I can't believe that really happened,' he said huskily. 'It was unbelievable.'

The green eyes glinted at him through their golden net of lashes. 'Are you complaining, Ashley?'

'No, you wasp-tongued seductress, I'm not,' he smiled, letting the hard mouth brush against her lips. 'Now tell me you love me.'

'Don't you know?' The green eyes opened to tease him. 'Wasn't I slightly obvious just now?'

'I want to hear you say it again,' he said softly.

'I love you, I love you, I love you,' she recited mockingly. 'Shall I write it out a hundred times?'

'Be careful,' he warned menacingly. 'You're very vulnerable at the moment, my darling. I shall never be tired of hearing you admit it.'

'I love you.' This time the words were groaned out against his warm skin, her kisses adoring him.

'Better,' he said thickly.

Her mouth incited him to kiss her, her lips gently raised to touch his in a ghost kiss, brushing him and moving away far enough for him to come down in hungry exploration once more.

As the kiss broke off he sighed. 'You're irresistible, you know that, don't you? Every man who looks at you has to want you.'

'Don't be silly,' she denied, with a shake of her head, fearing the rising of his jealousy again.

'Oh, yes,' he said obstinately. 'I'll never forget what Ravern said about being unable to get you out of his head. I knew what he meant. You're a walking invitation to any man you meet. Even when you were encased in ice you only had to smile and I would feel my temperature rising.'

Selina smiled. 'Is it rising now?'

'Can't you feel it?' he asked huskily.

'Can't you feel my heart beating?' she counter-attacked.

He deliberately laid his hand on the swiftly rising and falling white swell of her breast, and she moaned, her eyes closing in instant surrender.

'I love you,' he muttered hoarsely. 'Oh, God, I love you.'

'Don't make it sound like a death sentence,' she said lightly, trying to smile but moved by the passion in his voice.

'It's a life sentence,' he said, trying to lighten his own tone. 'If you knew how jealous I was of Ravern that evening ... I was so terrified you might be attracted to him.'

'How could you think that, Ashley?' She was half

annoyed, but her eyes mocked him. 'Don't tell me you don't know you're much sexier!'

'Don't make fun of me, damn you,' he said, but he laughed. 'So you don't fancy Sir Daniel? Are you quite sure?'

'I had a slight hang-up about him because of the trial,' she admitted. 'When I saw him again I suppose I remembered that, but I was too much yours to ever feel attracted to any other man.'

'Mine?' His voice groaned out the word. 'Are you, Selina? Mine? Completely mine?'

'If you aren't certain of that by now perhaps you'd like me to prove it all over again?' she whispered, her smile teasing and inviting.

'I'll take you up on that offer later,' he threatened, his grey eyes smouldering at her. 'God, darling, you don't know how terrified I've been in the last fortnight. I was so afraid you would disappear again. I was jealous of every man who saw you, every man you smiled at ... Hell, I was even jealous of the way you smiled at Stow tonight!'

'Oh, Ashley, how can you be so absurd?' Her eyes danced in light amusement. 'Stow? Your man of all trades, who hates women?'

'Even Stow found you irresistible,' he said obstinately. 'I've never seen him so taken by a member of the opposite sex. He was positively fatherly towards you. Usually he treats all women with a mixture of icy contempt and indifference. When I came back and heard you laughing and saw Stow smiling at you so indulgently, I almost blew a blood vessel. It may be idiotic, but I wanted all your smiles, all your laughter ...' His breath caught and his hand curved possessively around her long pale throat.

'What are you going to do now? Strangle me?' she asked him lightly, quite unafraid.

'I used to consider it,' he admitted huskily, his fingers involuntarily tightening. 'There were a hundred different deaths I planned for you during the three long years we were apart, but all of them somehow ended in my possessing you and feeling you yield passionately.' He smiled tautly, the long fingers relaxing in order to caress her throat. 'I warned you I was insane, a monomaniac whose obsession was a driving desire to possess you.'

'And now you have,' she murmured.

Ashley's eyes flared darkly. 'Now I have,' he agreed in a voice which made her heart turn over.

'So now you're satisfied?' she asked with a teasing flicker of her lashes, half afraid even now of the violent passion she saw in those grey eyes.

'As if you didn't know the answer to that one!' His voice was grim as he sent a long hard look over her.

'You told me that once you were satisfied you would no longer want me,' she pointed out, her eyes demurely lowered.

'I lied, damn you,' he said half savagely. 'I wanted to punish you for the agony you'd caused me. I think I really was a little mad for a while. But whatever I said then, I was crazy about you. I was even jealous of that young fool who claimed to know Roger ... in my right mind I would never have given him a second thought. But insecurity makes one violent. You smiled at him and I went up like straw. Given half a chance I'd have killed the brash idiot.' His brown hand tightened on her throat. 'And then killed you.'

Something of her old fear of him returned, and she looked at him doubtfully. 'Would you?' The savagery was not dead in him and it alarmed her still.

His mouth contorted in self-derision. 'After making love to you for days, perhaps,' he said thickly. 'Weeks, years ...' His hand moved down her throat in a slow caress, his eyes eating her. 'I don't think you realise how much I want you, Selina. You smile and my blood turns to fire. You've put me through hell ever since we met, but I can't uproot you from my heart. I tried, God knows. I had a few months of insanity when I tried to forget you with a dozen different women ...'

'Oh, did you?' she asked, her voice harsh with pain.

His smile was tender. 'Oh, I tried, Selina, but you haunted me. In the end I admitted it to myself and gave up fighting it. I lived for the damned reports that detective sent me. Across the Atlantic I read every detail of your daily life as though it were the Bible. I coveted every scrap of information I could get. I fought against a need to see you again.' His eyes flashed. 'I even had the man take pictures of you secretly ... I've kept them all. I used to stare at them endlessly. I papered my bedroom with them. You seemed to get lovelier with every month.'

She was so dumbfounded she could only stare at him. 'Pictures of me doing what?'

'Shopping, singing, walking ...' He shrugged. 'Everything and anything. The fellow thought I was a lunatic. God knows what he thought I was planning ... a kidnap, possibly. Or some sort of nasty revenge. He knew you were my wife once, of course.'

'Oh, Ashley,' she sighed, moved by these new revelations.

He kissed her hard and briefly. 'I don't suppose you even thought of me once ...' But the grey eyes watched her eagerly as he put the question in a careless tone.

She ran her fingertips around the hard lines of his face. 'I thought of very little else,' she admitted gently. 'When I heard you were dead I almost died myself. It was the most appalling shock to see you across the club that night. I thought I was seeing things ... my sub-conscious conjuring you up to comfort me ...'

'I want you to have suffered a little,' he said, lifting her hands and pressing his mouth in turn to the centre of each soft palm. 'It seems only fair.'

'If only I'd told you the truth when we first met,' she said, on a long sigh.

'When I was temporarily sane from time to time I realised there had to be a reason why you were so petri-fied of sex. I had my detective investigate your past, but he came up against a blank wall. He couldn't trace you past your debut at Freddie's Place because you'd changed your name.'

'I didn't dare risk the authorities finding us and taking Roger away from me. They wouldn't have ap-proved of a child of his age being brought up by a sixteen-year-old girl who was singing in a night club. Luckily I was able to pass for nineteen with good make-up, and with Freddie's help I was able to keep out of trouble.'

'We must deal with Roger when we get back to nor-mal,' Ashley said quietly. 'That young man needs a firmer hand than yours, Selina.'

She looked at him anxiously. 'He had a terrible childhood, Ashley ...'

'I know,' he said gently. 'But like you, my darling, he has to grow up some time. Will you trust me with him?'

Selina leant her head against him confidingly. 'I trust you utterly,' she said.

The dark mask of his face tightened. 'Oh, God, I love you,' he said with such grinding passion that her heart began to race again, his mouth seeking and finding hers in a kiss which was an act of possession as deep and total as the earlier act of love. She gave herself to him without reserve, meeting the flame of his passion with her own, her pulses racing as she felt his body shake in response.

'Will you forgive me my cruelty on our honeymoon?' he asked her tenderly afterwards. 'I meant to be patient, God knows. I lost my head every time I was near you. I was starving for you. You were so lovely I would have destroyed myself to get you, but I never meant to destroy you.'

'For a few hours after the first time I hated you,' she admitted. 'But I loved you too, so much that I knew, deep inside me, that I'd wanted it as much as you did, and that mutual desire was what love was all about. I can't pretend I wasn't frightened ... I was, darling, but I wanted you to make love to me again. I think I was half cured when I heard you were dead. The shock, the finality, of it was cauterising. I'd always wanted you, but I'd been so afraid. When I thought I would never be able to touch you again I knew that even fear wasn't as strong as love ...'

'But when you saw me again you still fought me,' he protested, staring at her with a frown.

She shrugged helplessly. 'I know. I think that was the last few barriers putting up a struggle. Once you'd actually made love to me, and I'd realised it wasn't so terrifying after all, they went down with a crash, especially as you hadn't been shocked and repelled by what you'd heard about the past, as I'd thought you would be ... it was partly because I couldn't bear the thought of you knowing all that, that I was afraid to let myself go with you ...'

'You crazy woman,' Ashley murmured, his eyes tender. 'You couldn't drive me away from you if you tried, so you'd better not ever try. Nothing is ever going to come between us again. I've got you now, and I mean to keep you. For the rest of your life you're going to make it up to me.'

'Then I'd better start now,' Selina said contentedly, offering herself without fear to those demanding arms.